Silas Snobden's
Office Boy

Horatio Alger, Jr.

Silas Snobden's
Office Boy

FOREWORD BY RALPH D. GARDNER

1973
Doubleday & Company, Inc.
Garden City, New York

ISBN: 0-385-02551-3
Library of Congress Catalog Card Number 72–87500
Foreword Copyright © 1973 by Doubleday & Company, Inc.
Printed in the United States of America
First Edition

FOREWORD:

A NEW BOOK BY HORATIO ALGER!

A new book by Horatio Alger!

What a thrill that announcement brought to now-grayed or graying old-timers who were youngsters a couple of generations (and longer) ago. It stirs recollections of favorite story titles, daring adventures and satisfying, sigh-of-relief conclusions with villains thwarted, the old homestead saved and Our Hero well launched upon the road to success.

The Alger Hero, as a matter of fact, has become a part of our language. As a synonym for spectacular rise to fame and wealth it has an immediate sight identification that few, if any, other names imply. For who, upon hearing the phrase, "a typical Alger Hero," does not immediately anticipate a report on the uniquely American phenomenon of one who started from scratch and—generally against great odds—reached the top rung of the ladder?

Isn't it strange, then, that so little is known today about Horatio Alger and his works?

In lectures to American Studies groups at various universities, I often start with a question: "Who was Horatio Alger?"

"A poor boy who worked hard and grew up to become a millionaire."

"The name of the hero of a long series of stories."

"A pen-name of Charles Dickens."

Although some know the answer, replies frequently fall short of the target. Rest assured that Horatio Alger was the real name of a real person. Born at Chelsea,[1] Massachusetts, on Friday, January 13, 1832, he authored more than one hundred stories[2] that were printed in scores of editions and multi-millions of copies during the half-century between our Civil War and World War I. Even after his death in 1899, Alger titles were being read and reread, bought, borrowed and swapped. Libraries displayed double rows of these fast-moving adventure tales. They were favorite gifts, awarded as school prizes and recommended in sermons. It is safe to assume that there was a very long period during which most boys—and many girls— who were brought up in the United States enjoyed Alger. He was, without doubt, America's all-time best-selling author!

But there are critics who protest that Horatio Alger was an overrated fraud. He mislead kids, they claim, probably causing many who stood up to the neighborhood bully to wind up with a bloody nose. Paul Gallico once wrote that Alger so frightened children with threats of the sinister village squire foreclosing the mortgage that they grew up fearful of mortgages although they didn't really know why they were afraid, or what they were afraid of.

We hear from some whose comments are even more crushing. They cling to the fiction that, after a heartbreaking college romance that was shattered by his father, Alger rebounded to become a mid-Victorian playboy who chased a Parisian cabaret singer and an English hussy through the hills of Montmartre. In later years, their fantasy persists, he was a pathetically inept adulterer. This may be the stuff from which more recent anti-hero tales are made, but it is contradicted by facts.[3]

Records indicate, rather, that Horatio Alger, Jr.—he always signed his name that way—was the oldest of five children of a debt-ridden New England parson. A sickly infant affected all his life by bronchial asthma, he couldn't talk until his seventh year. Nevertheless, he became an honor student at Harvard, a magazine and newspaper editor in Boston, and a teacher.[4] After graduating from the Divinity School at Cambridge, in 1860, he traveled to Europe as a correspondent for the New York *Sun* and the Boston *Transcript*. Returning shortly after the attack upon Fort Sumter, Alger tried to enlist in the Union Army but, due to his bronchial condition (and perhaps, too, because he stood only slightly over five feet tall), was three times rejected. Halfheartedly, he then accepted the pulpit of the First Parish Unitarian Church at Brewster, Massachusetts, resigning less than two years later and moving to New York to pursue a full-time career as a writer.[5]

Since his Harvard days, when he was both a student and disciple of Henry Wadsworth Longfellow, he submitted dozens of bittersweet poems to then popular periodicals.[6] Finding the poetry market limited, he turned to short stories, encouraged by William T. Adams who, as Oliver Optic, was an author and the editor of *Student And Schoolmate*, the monthly in which *Ragged Dick* was serialized in 1867.

Ragged Dick; or, Street Life in New York was not Alger's first book (it was his eighth), but it was the one that set the pattern for dozens of hero fiction plots he produced at the rate of three or four annually, over the next three decades. It was an overnight sensation and, when issued as a book the following year by the Boston publisher A. K. Loring established Horatio Alger as a major writer for young people.

Dick, a Huckleberry Finn of The Bowery, was a homeless bootblack. He gambled, swigged shots of whiskey at two cents a glass, relished an evening at Barnum's Museum or the Old Bowery Theatre and treated himself to a cigar when he had the extra penny to spare. Alger sometimes supplied such flaws to avoid crowning his lads with a halo or risking them being judged too good to be true. Needless to say, Dick reformed before many chapters pass. Then, defeating schemes of a variety of evil-doers, aided by kindly benefactors and with generous dollops of luck and pluck, he spun through a dozen adventures. By story's end, pleased with his self-improvement, a growing bank account and a good job, Dick told his chum, Fosdick, that he was keeping his box and brushes ". . . to remind me of the hard times I've had when I was an ignorant bootblack and never expected anything better."

"When, in short, you were 'Ragged Dick.' You must drop that name, and think of yourself now as—"

"Richard Hunter, Esq.," said our hero, smiling.

"A young gentleman on the way to fame and fortune," added Fosdick.

Dick's friends were then invited to follow his progress in *Fame And Fortune*, the second volume of the series.

Although Alger—who made no pretense to literary genius—wove these stories from similar fabric, he altered patterns sufficiently to keep his readers happily anticipating the next arrival. Actually, he employed four basic themes.

There was, like Ragged Dick, the city waif—an orphan of uncertain background. There was the recently orphaned country boy forced to leave home to seek his fortune in the city. Alger varied some narratives with the addition of a careworn, widowed mother and sometimes a dependent brother or sister. Several heroes were kidnapped in infancy from wealthy homes and loving parents to be reared as tramps, slum urchins or poorhouse scullions. Of course, they ultimately learned their true identities. In any number of these stories a culprit was trying to swindle the hero of an inheritance, usually mining or railroad stocks.

Alger liked to describe his young men as being about sixteen years old, not handsome but physically attractive. Hector Roscoe, in *Hector's Inheritance*, was "slenderly but strongly made, with a clear skin and dark eyes and a straightforward look. He had a winning smile that attracted all who saw it, but his face could assume a different expression, if need be. There were strong lines around his mouth that indicated calm resolution and strength of purpose. He was not a boy who would allow himself to be imposed upon, but was properly tenacious of his rights." Scott Walton, in *The Young Salesman,* was "the picture of health. He was inclined to be dark, with black hair, bright eyes, and with considerable color in his cheeks." Ben Stanton, *The Young Explorer,* was "strong and self-reliant . . . his limbs active, and his face ruddy with health. He looked like a boy who could get along. He was not a sensitive plant, and not to be discouraged by rebuffs."

Alger designed his hero as the boy he wished he, himself, could have been. They often were dark complexioned, described as "swarthy." Besides fictional characters, he portrayed Daniel Webster and Abraham Lincoln as swarthy in his biographies of them.

Alger customarily thrust the hero upon Lower Broadway with but a few cents in his pocket. Though ragged, he was bright, ambitious and aggressive and cheerfully accepted a menial station as bootblack, newsboy or peddler. From the beginning he had enemies—the swaggering snob, the criminally inclined guardian, the street-corner bully, the traveling conman, the pickpocket, burglar and kidnapper.

Scoundrels conspired to waylay the hero by chloroform, slugging, drugging or shanghaiing. They tried to steal his wallet, and he was occasionally thrown into an abandoned well. Between daring escapes he performed heroic deeds, rescuing a child from the path of a runaway horse, jumping into the East River to save a life, flagging down a speeding train or preventing an old man from being blackjacked and robbed.

He was rewarded with cash (which was wisely invested) and a better job, perhaps as a clerk earning as much as ten dollars a week. Because he showed initiative and shrewdness, he was sent on a confidential and perilous journey. This mission was always a triumph and in its course he may have discovered some secret that cleared up the mystery of his own identity, or accidentally met the man who helped recover his legacy. While the hero most often had not achieved great wealth, he was well on his way with the clouds past and a bright future predicted at the inevitable happy ending.

Alger was partial to alliterative titles, some of his most popular being *Sink Or Swim, Try And Trust, Rough And Ready, Brave And Bold, Slow And Sure* and *Strive And Succeed*. Heroes were named Frank Fowler, Mark Mason, Bob Burton and Tom Tracy. There were more than a hundred of them, and they all strived and succeeded.

Horatio Alger's literary quality, modern critics complain, was meager, to say the least. The Alger Hero often was cloyingly virtuous, his rise from rags to riches too often based upon incredible luck. And all he ever cared about was making money! Without attempting to equate Alger's unique product with that of a Herman Melville, a Nathaniel Hawthorne or a Stephen Crane, it is reasonable to suggest that millions who were enchanted by his stories in times gone by would disagree. Too often his works are examined in the light of late twentieth-century standards, and in Alger's case, such judgment may be inappropriate. During the 1860s and '70s our ancestors readily accepted slower-moving vehicles than the jet aircraft we now use. We wouldn't plan a trip in those fragile covered wagons or buggies, but in their own time they were considered dependable, practical ways to travel. Evaluating Horatio Alger's unsophisticated museum pieces by current rules is about the same as judging horse-drawn shays by criteria set for jet aircraft.

In any event, there seem to be no lack of diverging opinions. Russel Crouse called these works "literary murder," while a New York *Times* editorial named Alger "the Prose Laureate" of juvenile writers. Westbrook Pegler denounced Alger's heroes as "sanctimonious little heels," but Heywood Broun admired these "simple tales of honesty triumphant." S. N. Behrman, rediscovering an Alger story he had cherished years before, simply declared: "I don't know any comparable reading experience; it is like taking a shower in sheer innocence."[7]

Some complaints, however, are fair enough. Alger's writing was careless. He misplaced characters and committed frequent errors. Considering the pace at which he worked—generally composing two or three stories at the same time—mistakes are not surprising. One of his speediest assignments was *From Canal Boy To President*, a biography of James A. Garfield, which the publisher wished to distribute as quickly as possible after the assassination. With little more than newspaper obituary notices before him, Alger loosely assembled the facts, producing in three weeks another typical success story with President Garfield as its hero. In his introduction, Alger recommended two other books where more reliable information was obtainable.

Haste was also apparent in *Charlie Codman's Cruise*, in which Bertha Bowman, "a young lady of ten, with mirthful black eyes and very red cheeks," was mentioned as Ida. Ida actually was the foundling of *Timothy Crump's Ward*, which was concurrently in progress. To balance the scales, Alger referred to Mr. Crump as Mr. Cooper.

In *The Western Boy*, a character introduced as a police officer was, lower on the same page, a physician. Philip Gray's uncle, who disappeared early in *The Young Musician*, was left noticeably unaccounted for. And after telling us that *Tattered Tom* (who was a girl) was really named Jane, Alger called her Jenny. In the same book, Miss Sue Cameron suddenly was known as Mrs. Cameron without explanation or benefit of clergy.*

Alger was clumsiest when it came to romance, a subject he generally avoided. When inadvertently brushing up against intimacy, he became entangled in double entendre that, even in his day, must have raised eyebrows. For instance, Jasper Kent, in *Frank And Fearless*, was the prisoner of a band of outlaws.

* A half dozen of these Algerisms appear in *Silas Snobden's Office Boy*. How many can you find?

He heard footsteps and supposed it to be "the old man with his dinner." Instead, "he beheld the fresh face of a young girl, apparently about sixteen years of age." Leaving his food and saying she would return later with supper, Alger exclaimed, "She left Jasper eager and excited!" When the hero of *Tom Temple's Career* was the guest of Imogene Davenport, she declared "I want to show you some engravings." A few sentences later Alger confided that "Imogene laid herself out to entertain him, and at all events succeeded in monopolizing his attention." As Miss Pendleton, an aging spinster in *Sink Or Swim*, was about to start a vacation, the author revealed that she looked forward to "intercourse which her mode of life for many years had rendered impracticable."

His incredible naïveté notwithstanding, few will disagree that Horatio Alger was a novelist of tremendous influence. For youngsters on farms and in teeming cities he provided repeatedly acknowledged incentives to struggle upward. His stories' magic effect upon many was their own resolve that "If Ragged Dick could do it, so can I!" And those who made their dreams come true often credit the little minister's help.

Benjamin Fairless, who rose in life from a part-time school teacher to head United States Steel, collected Algers in his youth. Former New York Governor Alfred E. Smith bought the cheap paperback copies while still a newsboy on Manhattan's Lower East Side. Carl Sandburg recalled the good supply at the public library near his Galesburg, Illinois, home. Herbert H. Lehman, a banker, former Governor of New York and United States Senator, knew Alger personally. He "eagerly awaited the publication of every book Alger wrote."

Francis Cardinal Spellman, former Archbishop of New York, as a boy sought them at the Whitman, Massachusetts, Public Library. "I read all that were available," he wrote, "and enjoyed and, I am sure, benefited from reading them." James A. Farley, Board Chairman of Coca-Cola Export Corporation and former United States Postmaster General, read Algers when these

books were as much a part of our scene as county fairs and
Fourth of July concerts. Joyce Kilmer read Alger. So did Ernest
Hemingway and F. Scott Fitzgerald.

On at least two occasions Horatio Alger's influential pen
attracted considerable attention to urgent social needs. His
unliterary but graphic exposé of the cruel padrone system broke
the back of that racket in New York and other major cities.
In 1872 he dramatically chronicled this crime in *Phil The Fiddler*, one of his best and most beloved works.

That story described how boys and girls were taken (sometimes bought) from their impoverished homes in Southern
Italy, parents deceived that they were being brought to a better life. Once arrived here, they were sent into the streets as
beggars or musicians, often trained as pickpockets and thieves.
Subjected to inhuman treatment by severe masters, their mor-
tality rate was high, the entire outrage scandalous. But until
Horatio Alger seized the initiative, leading the drive against
this slavery, official policy was to keep hands off and look the
other way.

It took Alger only six months after publication of *Phil The
Fiddler* to doom this criminal traffic. Although his life was
repeatedly threatened and he even was mauled by irate padrones,
he stuck to his guns—and won. The story of Phil provided the
needed stimulus, forcing New York State legislators to enact
into law the prevention of cruelty to children.

Julius; or, The Street Boy Out West, published in 1874,
became another powerful document. The book drummed up
considerable public interest in the Children's Aid Society's
project to take thousands of homeless waifs off city streets and
transport them halfway across the continent, where their new
foster families were establishing homes along the recently
opened frontier.

Several years later he became interested in the Fresh Air
Fund, a project sponsored by his friend, Whitelaw Reid, who
was then owner of the New York *Tribune*. Alger pledged whole-

hearted efforts to this program and helped to provide slum children with country vacations.

These achievements are long forgotten. But he is still remembered—critically by some; with nostalgic reverence by others—for his stories. And these are often referred to as "algers." "This use of a proper noun as if it were a common one is associated with very few other authors," wrote Clifton Fadiman. "One does not buy a few balzacs or a couple of hemingways. But an alger is a *thing*."[8]

While mocking Alger's style is easy, and occasional articles—by writers who take him much too seriously—appear to aim in that direction, it is to reckon without the experts. The Selection Committee for the Grolier Club's monumental 1946 exhibition of One Hundred Influential American Books Printed Before 1900 voted *Ragged Dick* "sufficiently Grade A" for inclusion. Frank Luther Mott, in *Golden Multitudes; the Story of Best Sellers in the United States,* also named *Ragged Dick* in the column of Over-All Best Sellers. Three others—*Fame And Fortune, Luck And Pluck* and *Tattered Tom*—won positions on his runner-up roster of Better Sellers. The durability of both Dick and Tom was again recognized in *Peter Parley to Penrod,* Jacob Blanck's bibliographical description of best-loved American juvenile books.

Try to ascertain how many of Alger's books were printed during his long reign and you'll come up with astonishing numbers. Although his popularity began to wane during World War I, his books remained in print, profusely, through the 1920s. Street & Smith continued their long-running Alger Series, listing some forty titles, well into the thirties. Estimated totals range from a high of 400,000,000—a figure that is questioned—downwards to the 250,000,000 claimed by Quentin Reynolds in his history of Street & Smith; the 200,000,000 quoted in a New York *Times Magazine* article or the relatively modest 100,000,000 copies suggested by Frederick Lewis Allen. Because most of Alger's more than five dozen publishers went out of business years ago, the exact quantity will never be known. But even the most conservative of these estimates would still be phenomenal![9]

To more fully understand the magic appeal of Horatio Alger's stories, it is necessary to explore—from the contemporary point of view—some alternatives and what preceded them.

Some forty years before *Ragged Dick*, Samuel Griswold Goodrich began writing 100-plus *Tales of Peter Parley*, possibly the earliest of this country's juveniles that were not heavily weighted with religious or moral lessons. It was a start. During the 1830s, the Rev. Jacob Abbott launched his Rollo series about a good little boy, extraordinarily inquisitive, who never soiled his starched white collar, whether digging a ditch or climbing a tree. Kids accepted Rollo, but there was little there to set the juices flowing.

By 1852 the outlook brightened with publication of Nathaniel Hawthorne's first *Wonder Book*. Three years later, Oliver Optic's *The Boat Club* appeared. This introduced a long succession which, while bearing occasional similarity to those turned out by Alger, never quite attained Alger's eminence.

Then, in June 1860 the firm of Erastus F. Beadle issued *Malaeska: The Indian Wife of the White Hunter* by Ann S. Stephens. Its popularity created a demand for these sensational "yellow-backs," our first genuinely native form of literature. Recounting daring exploits of swashbuckling adventurers, these small paperback dime novels were loaded with action and vivid descriptions of mayhem, Indian raids and life in the wilds. Quickly detecting a trend, other publishers issued blood-and-thunder tales of Kit Carson, Buffalo Bill, Texas Jack and other famed scouts. Covers featured by-lines of Edward S. Ellis, Ned Buntline (E. Z. C. Judson), Col. Prentiss Ingraham, Gilbert Patten (who later, as Burt L. Standish, originated Frank Merriwell) and a vast army of swift writers well equipped with adjectives, heroic phrases and the ability to make readers tingle with excitement. These were lurid, illustrated with scenes of violence. They traveled with railroad construction crews and were carried South to Manassas, Shiloh and Vicksburg in knapsacks of Union troops throughout the Civil War. Boys loved the dime novels but had to read them clandestinely, for they were abhorred by parents and forbidden at home.

What about foreign authors? Charles Dickens masterfully described the plights of poverty, but generally without leading his fascinating characters to high reward. Hans Christian Andersen spun charming tales of the poor, but too often left children in tears. And the Brothers Grimm frightened kids out of their wits!

So it was left to Horatio Alger, who had not a small fraction of their talent, to concoct the formula that became as acceptable as it was durable. And it came at the right moment, for those were exciting, restless times, with soldiers of the North and the South returning home or seeking new roots. The nineteenth century still held more than thirty years of progress and invention and our nation continued expanding beyond the Great Plains.

Thousands flocked to cities from farms and small towns. Others envisioned new lives in the rich farmlands being opened to hardy settlers. Reports of gold and silver strikes beckoned from across the wilderness. Everywhere there was building. New industries developed. Items formerly crafted at home were now mass-produced in factories. In these unaccustomed surroundings, small children toiled alongside the men and women from early morning until dark.

America was experiencing unprecedented growth and opulence along with growing pains of depressions, panic and strife. And every day through our ports arrived the impoverished and oppressed of other lands. Throughout the country were the toiling, diligent many and the unscrupulous, tyrannical few. Between these groups were the weak, the confused and the innocent, sorely in need of a champion.

Consider, then, the opportune arrival of *Ragged Dick* and

the multitude of Alger heroes who followed. Here was action not previously found in "respectable" book form. These were adventures that kids craved and at the same time met with the hearty approval of parents. Not only were Alger's champions welcome indoors, but his books could be read in the parlor.

Although every story Horatio Alger wrote contained substantial doses of the didacticism of earlier writers, he—by intent or accident—fulfilled young people's needs and delights far better than his predecessors. He served up heroes with whom they identified, bullies they could whip and goals they believed they might attain. And he convinced them that—through honesty and clean living by the Golden Rule—riches and honor were within their reach; that any farm lad, newsboy or telegraph messenger could someday become President of the United States.

The American idea of success was not invented by Horatio Alger. It probably arrived with the earliest settlers and was later publicized by Benjamin Franklin. He prescribed thrift, industry and temperance. Alger adapted Franklin's principles, combined the basic plots of *Cinderella* and *Jack and the Beanstalk* and for many years remained the chief exponent of the Protestant Ethic.

Alger's advocacy was enhanced by an intimate familiarity with his subject and an energetic search for material. Shortly after arriving in New York he was taken to the Newsboys' Lodging House which, for six cents a night, was home and recreation center for hundreds of young street tradesmen. Alger established headquarters there, creating novels from the unending wealth of experiences described by the residents.[10]

Broadway, Wall Street, elegant homes near Madison Square and tenements of Mulberry Bend and the Five Points were familiar Alger settings, but—seeking new, authentic backgrounds—he traveled to Europe, dashed westward from Independence, Kansas, with a party of homesteaders, roamed through Indian country, visited mining camps in the California Sierras and sailed around Cape Horn in a four-masted schooner.

Like *Ragged Dick,* most of Horatio Alger's works were serialized in mass-circulation weekly and monthly periodicals before being issued as books. Serialization, during that period, generally represented the major portion of an author's compensation for a story. Book publication was a secondary benefit, with those rights often released for a flat fee. Purchase on a royalty basis depended upon the writer's prestige plus his acumen as a negotiator. Alger (who in recent years has inaccurately been labeled an unbusinesslike, impractical visionary), throughout his long career received top rates for serializations and royalties for books. He was also able to arrange contracts permitting him to write for a number of publishers simultaneously, favoring firms that issued to him stock in their corporations as a bonus.

So prolific was he that during eleven years after his death, sixteen accrued serializations made their appearance as bound volumes, still enthralling readers who enthusiastically responded to each announcement of "A New Book by Horatio Alger." *Robert Coverdale's Struggle,* when issued by Street & Smith, in 1910, was the last of these.

But today, more than fourscore years after its serialization in *The Argosy,* you are reading the bona fide first edition of *Silas Snobden's Office Boy, a new book by Horatio Alger!*

Frank Manton, Our Hero, was Silas Snobden's office boy, and one wonders where he's been all these years. While it would sap the combined talents of Old Sleuth and Nicholas Carter to track down enough leads to explain his strange disappearance, here is evidence to supply a partial solution:

A significant clue is that not a single one of this story's thirteen weekly installments showed the name of Horatio Alger as its author! From its beginning chapters, which appeared in the issue dated November 30, 1889, until its conclusion on

February 22, 1890, *Argosy* readers were advised that this rattling good yarn "issued from the pen of one of our most gifted contributors, Arthur Lee Putnam."

Arthur Lee Putnam?

Yes, and for good reason. Alger was grinding out so many *Argosy* serials that, between 1886 and 1893 he frequently had two in the same issue. For instance, when *Silas* began, final parts of *The Odds Against Him*, carrying the Alger by-line, were still appearing. A notice appended to its ending announced that *The Erie Train Boy*, "Mr. Alger's new story, will begin in next week's number."

To avoid confusion, and perhaps so as not to overwork the name of his star performer, publisher Frank A. Munsey devised the Putnam pseudonym. It appeared above not less than a dozen novels. When Putnam-signed serials were published as books, Alger became properly credited as their true creator.

Munsey intended to print this as *Mr. Snobden's Office Boy*, promoting it thusly in an advertisement. On the December 21, 1889 cover, the title was incorrectly displayed as *The Story of an Office Boy*.

Option to publish a bound volume was acquired in 1891 by the United States Book Company for inclusion in their Leather Clad Tales of Adventure and Romance Series. Reviving the unused Munsey title, *Mr. Snobden's Office Boy*, they copyrighted it as such with the Library of Congress. However, the firm went bankrupt that same year and the book was never issued.[11]

Curiously, that title had been registered in 1858 by the New York *Sun*, in which some of Alger's work was then being anonymously printed. There is no record that it ever appeared in that newspaper. If, indeed, this was the same story, then *The Argosy* text was substantially updated, for several references (concerning John L. Sullivan, Little Lord Fauntleroy, the kidnapped Charley Ross) had not yet occurred in 1858.

The Argosy was a thirty-two-page weekly story paper sold by subscription for five dollars per year, a steep price for those days. Munsey, describing his magazine, boasted it was "the cleanest and brightest of all the clever journals." He was fond of communicating with subscribers through an editorial page column. "Seven years ago," he wrote, "I came to New York from Maine, little more than a boy at the time . . . I had no capital to back my enterprise, and my friends all predicted utter failure." Doubtless, he fancied himself to be a real-life Alger hero.

He attracted first-class talent, paid well and invariably presented an impressive table of contents. The issues in which *Silas Snobden's Office Boy* appeared also featured (in addition to the two Alger-signed stories) *An Unprovoked Mutiny*, by James Otis; *Check 2134*, by Edward S. Ellis; *Among the Missing*, by Oliver Optic and *The Stolen Passports*, by William Murray Graydon. Every issue ran "a page of mirthful comics;" editorials on such current topics as "the late revolution in Brazil," a plan to "check runaway horses on the Brooklyn Bridge," how a life was saved "through an operation known as transfusion of blood," "a wild claim" that a Russian inventor has developed "a boat that is to move beneath the surface of the water," and that "While we in America are disputing which city shall obtain the honor of holding the World's Fair in 1892 to celebrate our discovery, Germany is quietly getting ready to astonish the universe with an exhibition which shall be a fair for the world in the most literal sense of the term."

There were articles about prominent persons whose accomplishments Munsey considered worth emulating. These included Cornelius Vanderbilt ("a wise head on young shoulders"); Representative William C. P. Breckenridge, of Kentucky ("a name to conjure with in the South"); Senator John C. Kenna, of West Virginia ("who began life as a farm boy") and Representative Byron M. Cutcheon, of Michigan ("His record in the war was a brilliant one").

In another department, brief answers were supplied to inquiries and opinions. Letter writers were advised that "there is

no premium on the half-dollar of 1830"; "Your suggestion of a
baseball league shall be carefully considered"; "the only way to
get work on a railroad is to apply to a railroad superintendent";
"Italy stands third in the list of naval powers" and "Jay Gould
is supposed to be worth about one hundred millions."

There were timely puzzles, often constructed around word
games. The issue of December 21, 1889 offered "The New Flag
Problem," which required some rearranging to accommodate
forty-two stars, including four new ones for recently admitted
North and South Dakota, Montana and Washington.

Advertisements were closely spaced on all four sides of the
magazine's dark orange covers, with relatively few inside. The
larger proportion touted miracle cures which would be banned
today and, in any event, seemed unsuited to *The Argosy's* generally youthful subscribers. There was Peck's Invisible Tubular
Ear Cushions to cure deafness and head noises. For fifty cents,
Dr. Dowd offered his "scientific method for developing plump,
rosy cheeks as well as every muscle of the limbs and body."
Piso's Cure was recommended as the best cough medicine for
consumption. While Scott's Emulsion's comparatively modest
promise was "Gain one pound a day" and Dr. Baker's Magnetic
Liniment was merely a "marvelous cure for rheumatic suf-
ferers," Dr. Kline's Great Nerve Restorer unreservedly guaranteed "all fits stopped after first day's use. $2.00 trial bottle free
to fit cases." Bruceline Hair Tonic "restores gray hair to its
original color; strengthens the hair, prevents it from falling out
and is guaranteed to produce a new growth." Hood's Sarsa-
parilla healed la grippe, headaches, rheumatism, malaria,
scrofula sores and catarrh "as it purifies the blood." It also ban-
ished such "agonies experienced by the dyspeptic as distress before or after eating, loss of appetite, irregularities of the
bowels, wind or gas pain, heartburn, sour stomach, mental de-
pression, nervous irritability and sleeplessness. 100 doses, One
Dollar."

Probably more interesting to young readers were Kelsey's

$3 Printing Press, The Complete Morse Telegraph Outfit, $3.75; Anthony's Champion Photographic Kit which, for $10, included a "handsome mahogany camera, fine acromatic lens, double dry plate holder and improved folding tripod." The New Vineyard 50-inch front-wheeled bicycle, worth $55, was offered for $32 on easy payments. There were "magic lanterns and stereopticons for public exhibitions and home amusement . . . A very profitable business for a man with small capital." The equipment included "scenery, comic and Bible views."

Other business opportunities were placed by the Grannan Detective Bureau Co., of Cincinnati, seeking "detectives in every county . . . shrewd men to act under instructions in our secret service. Experience not necessary. Send 2¢ stamp." The Mutual Helper Co., of Zanesville, Ohio, sought "a reliable man . . . sharp, shrewd and used to trading. The right party will be furnished with money to hire a horse and buggy . . ." The Curtis Publishing Company invited readers to earn big profits as sales agents and, in every issue, *The Argosy* told how to make two dollars on every subscription sent in, listing as added incentives a set of books written by Frank Munsey, an all-iron Rogers foot power scroll saw and the Celebrated Goodwell Lathe.

Confederate currency was offered for sale—$210 worth for $.25; twenty actress photos—"full length beauties"—cost $.04; Plymouth Rock pants, of Boston, were cut to order for $3; "a beautiful, useful and ornamental 1890 calendar would be sent for eight $.02 stamps; Sheridan's Condition Powder guaranteed to make hens lay, and free information was available on immigration to Oregon.

It is fairly certain that Horatio Alger was the most popular of *The Argosy's* contributors during his years of association with Munsey. More of his stories were printed than those of other authors, and the Alger (and Putnam) titles headed listings of contents.

While reading *Silas Snobden's Office Boy* let your imagination carry you back to an age when the pace was slower, skylines lower and the air sweeter. You'll like most of the people to be met here—sixteen-year-old Frank, with his "bright face and pleasant manner," who supports his widowed mother (she sews for $.25 a day), and Frank's odd-assorted lot of greater or lesser benefactors. These include the generous Allen Palmer ("who was handsomely dressed and had that quiet air of authority which comes from acknowledged position") and Samuel Graham (Frank returned his lost wallet), the aged eccentric who Alger says looks like Horace Greeley and is writing a history of the Saracens. Don't overlook Stasia Jane (although a "slatternly ragbag" of a drudge, she aids Frank in his search for Rob Palmer), Seth Hastings, the muscular milkman and all the others.

You are entitled to despise the villains, whom you'll recognize on sight. John Carter is a man with "a rakish air, whose mottled face and complexion of an unhealthy red, indicated intemperate habits." Luke Gerrish, who is also intemperate, possesses "a pair of eyes unusually small." And Gideon Chapin ("a sly, crafty man, who was not above misrepresentation if it would accomplish his purpose") rubs his hands while addressing his employer "in a cringing manner."

Then, of course, there is Silas Snobden, himself—the irritable, tight-fisted commission merchant of White Street—who, in the end, turns out to be not such a harsh fellow, after all.

You'll travel through New York as it used to be, enthusiastically escorted by the author. Horatio Alger will guide you uptown on the elevated railroad to the three-room Manton flat in West 31st Street, then on a perilous walk along Seventh Avenue. That neighborhood, Alger warns in a Baedeker-like description, "possessed an unenviable notoriety as the promenade of gangs of ruffianly men and boys, whose delight it is to attack and rob peaceable wayfarers." In contrast, he points out Mr. Palmer's residence, a "handsome brownstone dwelling four stories in height," located in West 48th Street, near Fifth Avenue.

You may follow Frank down Broadway to "a large clothing emporium," then crosstown to Mr. Graham's Clinton Street boardinghouse. There will be glimpses of the green at 42d Street and Sixth Avenue, then known as Reservoir Park, not far from the Astor Library and the once elegant but long-vanished Sturtevant House and Metropolitan Hotel.

Pause briefly to rest on a bench in quiet Madison Square before taking the Sixth Avenue horsecar to Christopher Street where the abducted little Rob is imprisoned in "a shabby house not far from the river." In his small room he "had no amusement except watching from the solitary window a goat disporting himself in the back yard." Alger takes you there, too, then hurries with you to the Hudson River pier to board the day boat for an eventful trip to Albany. At that time, he notes, the nine-hour voyage cost one dollar.

Read *Silas Snobden's Office Boy* for fun. You are going to enjoy this excursion into the tranquil, uncomplicated world of Horatio Alger. It may be the renewal of a happy old acquaintance or the start of a new one. It probably will not make you rich. It may not even get you started up the road to success. On the other hand, it may.

Ralph D. Gardner

New York

1. "Boy, you are my prisoner!" said the policeman as he laid his hand firmly on Frank's shoulder.

2. "Say, boy, don't be in such a hurry."

3. "So! The boy confesses!" said
Chapin, triumphantly.

4. "Read that, Frank, it is from
your Uncle George."

5. "I've had nothing to eat today."

6. "What are you here for?" asked Carter.

7. "I think, my dear, I'll trouble you to let me have half a dollar."

8. Trying to identify Luke Gerrish.

1. Now Revere.
2. Ralph D. Gardner, *Road to Success; The Bibliography of the Works of Horatio Alger* (Mendota, Ill.: Wayside Press, 1971). A total of 108 books, including the present volume, properly carry Alger's name as author (p. 14). After his death, eleven more were presented by Edward Stratemeyer, the famed writer of boys' books, who stated that these were completions of outlines Alger had left to him (p. 21).
3. Herbert R. Mayes, *Alger: A Biography Without a Hero* (New York: Macy-Masius, 1928). Mayes attributes these escapades to a diary he claims Alger started upon entering Harvard. As Mayes's book remained the only one on Alger until 1961, writers accepted and quoted its many errors. Some still do so, apparently preferring its contents to a number of less sensational but more reliable references now available.

   Malcolm Cowley appears to have been the first doubting scholar to question the authenticity of the diary. In "The Alger Story," *The New Republic*, (September 10, 1945), he writes: "Mayes says that much of his account was based on Alger's private diary, a black, clothbound volume; but in view of his other errors you can't help wondering whether he copied it correctly or whether it ever existed—for the diary has vanished since Mayes used it, and nobody else remembers having seen it." Frank Gruber, in *Horatio Alger, Jr.; A Biography and Bibliography of the Best Selling Author of All Time* (West Los Angeles: Grover Jones Press, 1961), p. 13, says: "Mayes' book is studded with such a vast number of factual errors and flights of imagination that I am compelled to discard virtually everything in the book with one single exception, the date of his birth. Even the date of his death is wrong." John Seelye, of the University of Connecticut, offers the most careful study to date of published Alger biographies. In "Who Was Horatio? The Alger Myth and American Scholarship," *American Quarterly*, Winter, 1965, pp. [749]–756, he cites those who relied heavily upon Mayes as "perpetuating the hoax." Seelye adds: "The book suited the temper of the times, which assumed that 'Victorianism' was a symbol for prudery and hypocrisy, and which welcomed the revelations of debunking biographers. . . ." Dr. Richard M. Huber, Dean of Students, Hunter College, also commented on the Mayes version. In *The American Idea Of Success* (New York: McGraw-Hill, 1971), p. 45, he says: "He based important parts of the biography on Alger's private diary, which would have been revealing, except it was Mayes, not Alger, who wrote Alger's diary."
4. Ralph D. Gardner, *Horatio Alger; or, the American Hero Era* (Mendota, Ill.: Wayside Press, 1964). Teaching was almost as important to Alger as writing. After graduating from Harvard he taught at a district school in Marlborough, Massachusetts, for the 1852 summer term (p. 118),

becoming in 1854 an instructor of Greek and Latin at the Potowome Boarding School for Boys, at East Greenwich, Rhode Island (p. 121), remaining until 1856, when he took charge of the academy at Deerfield, Massachusetts, for the summer session (p. 124). Even after becoming a celebrated writer, he remained a tutor in the classics to children of prominent New York families (p. 200). The late United States Supreme Court Justice Benjamin N. Cardozo, whom Alger prepared for the examination for admission to Columbia University during 1883–84, became his most famous pupil. Young Cardozo achieved a near perfect score at age fourteen and was admitted to Columbia the following year (pp. 271–75).

5. Richard M. Huber, op. cit., pp. 45–46, 469–70. Dr. Huber writes that Alger resigned after being accused of a homosexual incident by a church-appointed committee, documenting this with excerpts from the 1866 records of the First Parish Unitarian Church at Brewster, Massachusetts.

6. Ralph D. Gardner, *Road to Success*, op. cit., pp. 139–53.

7. The comment of Russel Crouse appears in "Introduction" in "Horatio Alger, Jr.," *Struggling Upward and Other Works* (New York: Crown Publishers, 1945), p. vii; editorial, "Ragged Dick," The New York *Times* (n.d.); Westbrook Pegler and Heywood Broun, in Thomas Kelland, "Boys of Today Don't Know Alger," The New York *World-Telegram* (January 13, 1941); S. N. Behrman in "Two Algers," an introduction in "Horatio Alger, Jr.," *Strive and Succeed* (New York: Holt, Rinehart and Winston, 1967), p. x.

8. Clifton Fadiman, in "Party of One," *Holiday* Magazine (February 1957).

9. The 250,000,000 total is from Quentin Reynolds, *The Fiction Factory; or, From Pulp Row to Quality Street* (New York: Random House, 1955), p. 83. 200,000,000 is from Thomas Meehan, in "A Forgettable Centenary—Horatio Alger," The New York *Times Magazine* (June 29, 1964). 100,000,000 is from Frederick Lewis Allen, in "Horatio Alger, Jr.," The *Saturday Review* (September 1, 1945).

10. A lifelong bachelor, Alger appears to have centered his emotional life around these boys. He became their adviser, confessor and frequent soft touch for a loan. He helped them find better jobs. With his substantial earnings, he put a number of youths through Brooklyn Business College, even setting some of them up in business. He legally adopted at least two, naming them among his heirs. Fuller details in Ralph D. Gardner, *Horatio Alger*, op. cit., pp. 195–99, 201–3, 227–30, 262–77, 280.

11. Ralph D. Gardner, *Road to Success*, op. cit., pp. 113–14.

CHAPTER I.

MR. SNOBDEN'S OFFICE BOY.

"Mr. Snobden!"

It was the office boy who spoke, and the person addressed was his employer, senior partner of the firm of Snobden & Downs, commission merchants on White Street, not far from Broadway, New York.

"Eh?" returned the merchant sharply, looking up from a letter he was writing. "Oh, it's you, is it? What do you want?"

"Do you think you could raise my pay a little?"

Mr. Snobden frowned, for he was not a liberal man, and didn't like such applications.

"What do you get now?" he asked.

"Four dollars, sir."

"Four dollars! Are you not satisfied with four dollars?"

"I am not dissatisfied, sir, but I find it hard to get along."

"Then you are extravagant, recklessly extravagant. How old are you?"

"Sixteen."

"Do you know what wages I was getting at your age?"

"No, sir."

"I only received three dollars. I should have felt rich with four dollars."

"Perhaps you did not have a mother to help support."

"Can't help that! I have nothing to do with your mother," rejoined Mr. Snobden, querulously. He eyed Frank Manton disapprovingly, as if the latter were very much to blame for having such an incumbrance as a mother.

"Tell your mother to work," he continued, "and earn something."

"She does work, sir, harder than I," returned Frank, indignantly.

"I can easily believe that. You have a very easy place. I worked much harder at your age."

Frank was privately of opinion that his place was not so easy, nor the duties as light as his employer represented, but he did not think it politic to say so. There really seemed nothing for him to say, and he stood silent with a look of disappointment on his face.

"Do you think," he ventured to ask a little later, "that I shall soon be promoted?"

"Can't say! Business is very poor. I am not making a cent. Very likely you are making more than I."

This seemed very ludicrous to Frank, as he compared his almost penniless condition with that of his well fed and prosperous employer who lived as he knew (for he had been sent there on an errand) in a fine brown stone house up town. He was aware, however, that the merchant was in the habit of speaking in this way, particularly when any one in his employ asked for an increase of salary.

Frank turned to leave the office, for the business of the day was over, when his employer called him back.

"Stay," he said, "I have two letters to mail. You may take them down to the general post office, as they are important, and I want them to go as soon as possible."

"Very well, sir."

"Here is a nickel to pay you for your trouble."

Frank took the money and expressed his thanks, though he was privately of opinion that it was rather poor pay for the extra service required. He went out into the street, and turned in the direction of Broadway. Leaning against the building was a young man of perhaps twenty eight, with a rakish air, whose mottled face and complexion of an unhealthy red, indicated intemperate habits. Frank was about to pass him without special notice when the young man, stepping forward, placed his hand on the office boy's shoulder.

"Say, kid," he said familiarly, "don't be in such a hurry."

Frank turned and eyed the man suspiciously.

"I *am* in a hurry," he rejoined.

"Then I'll walk along with you. Are you workin' for old Snobden?"

"I am working for *Mr.* Snobden," replied Frank.

"*Mr.* Snobden, then. However, I have a right to speak of him without ceremony, for he is my uncle."

"Is that so?" asked Frank in surprise.

"Yes it is. I don't wonder you're surprised. I don't look over prosperous, do I?"

"No, you don't," answered the boy, taking note of the other's shabby coat, soiled vest and frayed pantaloons.

"Yet that man is my mother's brother—was, I mean, for the old lady is dead."

Frank was devotedly attached to his own mother, and this careless speech grated on his ear.

"Yet," continued the young man, "though I am poor and he is rolling in wealth, he won't do anything for me. What do you think of that?"

"Won't he hire you as clerk?"

"No; I've asked him, but he'd rather give his money to strangers than to one of his own kith and kin."

"I don't think I should care to employ you as clerk," thought Frank, and he was not disposed to criticise Mr. Snobden for declining to give a business position to the young man who walked beside him.

"What's your name?" he asked.

"John Carter."

"Then one of the letters I am carrying to the post office is for you."

"Is it?" asked the young man eagerly. "Then give it to me."

Frank drew back.

"I can't do it," he said.

"But I tell you the letter is for me. Let me see it."

Frank cautiously displayed the envelope containing the address.

Mr. John Carter.

No. 17 1-2 East Fourth Street.

City.

"Yes, that's where I live. Give it to me."

"Excuse me, but I am to carry these letters to the post office."

"Don't be ridiculous! The letter would come to me sooner or later."

"Very likely; but Mr. Snobden didn't authorize me to give it to a person in the street."

"You're a fool!" said Carter roughly. "What's the difference as long as it gets into the right hands?"

"How do I know that you are the man the letter is for?"

"Didn't I tell you my name is John Carter?"

"There may be more than one John Carter in the city."

"There is only one John Carter who lives in East Fourth Street," said the young man triumphantly.

"I don't know whether you live in East Fourth Street or not."

"Do you mean to insult me, kid?"

"I don't care to be called kid. No, I don't mean to insult you."

"You doubt my word."

"No, I don't, but as I don't know you, I can't tell whether you tell the truth or not."

They were now on Broadway, and gradually nearing the post office.

Carter watched to see if there was not an opportunity to

snatch the letter, but Frank had taken care to return it to his pocket.

"Look here," said Carter, "I'm in a hurry. That letter is very important to me. It probably contains money."

"Then it is all the more necessary that I should not give it up."

"Bosh!"

"What makes you think the letter contains money?"

"Because I wrote the old fellow that I was sick abed and hadn't a cent to buy food. He couldn't resist that, could he?" and Carter laughed noisily.

"But that was not true."

"Well, what's the odds if it wasn't? The old man is a miser with a heart like a flint, and you've got to hatch up some story like that. I do need the money bad enough, as you can see."

"Yes, you don't seem rich."

"Rich! I should say not. If brown stone houses were selling at fifty cents apiece I haven't got money enough to buy half a one."

"You don't look very rich, that's a fact."

"Then will you give me the letter?"

"No, we are close to the post office. I will deposit it, and then you can call for it."

"I shall have to wait until it is delivered at my lodging."

"I am sorry, but you will have to wait."

"Will you lend me a quarter till tomorrow? I will pay you from the money in the letter."

"I couldn't do it. I have no money to spare."

"Look here, young feller, you put on too many airs for an office boy. You know too much!"

Frank smiled.

"I wish I did," he replied. "I never thought I knew enough."

They entered the post office, and Frank, going up to one of the slits, dropped the two letters in.

CHAPTER II.

AN UNWELCOME LETTER.

"Well you've gone and done it," said Carter, provoked.

"I've done what I was sent to do."

"And I shan't get the letter till tomorrow morning."

"You might ask for it. If they will give it to you, it is none of my business."

John Carter decided to follow Frank's advice. He went up to the General Delivery, and said: "There is a letter for me. Please hand it to me."

"What is your name?"

"John Carter."

"I don't find any letter so addressed."

"It has just been put in."

"How do you know?"

"I saw a boy put it into the letter box."

The clerk began to look suspicious. Carter's appearance was not such as to inspire confidence.

"Do you know how it was addressed?"

"It was addressed to me at my residence, No. 17 1-2 East Fourth Street."

"Then it will be delivered there."

"But I shall have to wait for it. I would like to get it now."

"It would be against rules to deliver it."

"But——"

"Stand aside! You are interfering with others," said the clerk.

"There, kid," muttered Carter angrily, "you see what trouble you have made me."

"I am sorry, Mr. Carter, but duty required me to do as I did."

"Duty!" sneered Carter. "What an awfully good boy you are!"

"Thank you," returned Frank with a smile. "I am afraid I don't deserve the compliment."

"How long have you been working for my uncle?"

"Nine months."

"Does he pay you well?"

"I get four dollars a week."

"Do you like him?"

"I have no complaint to make," answered Frank cautiously, not caring to take Mr. Carter into his confidence.

"When does my uncle leave the office?"

"He generally stays after all the clerks are gone, and writes or looks after the accounts."

"He does, does he?" said Carter, looking interested. "When does the store close up?"

"At five o'clock just now—later some parts of the year."

"Humph! So the old man works longer than any of you."

"I would be willing to do the same if I had a business of my own."

"If I had a business of my own I'd hire others to do the work, and have a good time."

"I dare say you would," thought Frank. "That isn't the way to succeed."

As it was late Frank concluded to spend the nickel he had earned in riding up town on the elevated road.

He got off at the Thirty Third Street station, and walked across to a house on Thirty First Street between Seventh and Eighth Avenues. He entered a large tenement house, and walked up to the third landing. He opened a door on the left, and found himself in a small suite of three rooms. The table was set in the largest one, and his mother was toasting bread at the stove.

She was a pleasant looking woman, not far from forty.

"I am glad to see you, Frank," she said. "Supper is about ready. Did you have to work hard today?"

"About the same as usual, mother. I had considerable walking to do. It seems good to sit down."

"I wish I could afford to send you to school instead of keeping you in business."

"It's all right, mother. I am satisfied, but I wish I were earning a larger salary. I haven't been raised since I went to work nine months ago."

"You might ask Mr. Snobden for a raise."

"I asked him tonight."

"What did he say?"

"That four dollars was a large salary, and I must be extravagant to want more."

"You extravagant! Poor Frank! You keep nothing for yourself, but hand all your wages to me."

"That is what I should do if I earned more. I don't care for that. I want you to be comfortable. Mother, do you know your dress is looking old and shabby?"

"I don't go much into society," said his mother cheerfully, "so I don't require fashionable clothes."

"I wish I could earn a little extra so as to buy you a new dress."

"Don't think of me! You need a new suit yourself, Frank."

"I can say the same as you—I don't go into society."

"But you need to dress well at your work."

Frank did not deny this, for he felt that he did need a new suit, and he had had more than one hint on the subject from his fellow clerks, who took him to task as a miser, and said he did no credit to the establishment.

"It'll come in time," he answered with affected cheerfulness. "Now let us sit down to supper."

The supper was plain, but good, and Frank, being gifted with a boy's healthy appetite, enjoyed it. He could have eaten more, but did not care to let his mother know this.

When supper was over, his mother said: "If you are not too tired, Frank, I should like to have you carry some work home for me."

"Certainly, mother. Where to?"

"Forty Ninth Street near Eighth Avenue. Mrs. Bond's."

"Have you the bundle ready?"

"Here it is."

"How much am I to collect?"

"A dollar and a half."

"Very well."

"You know our rent is due at the end of the week, and we shall need all we can collect."

Frank was about to start on his errand when at the door he met the postman.

"Any letters for us?" he asked pleasantly for he knew the mailcarrier, who lived in a neighboring street.

"No, Frank. Is there a Mrs. Gerrish who lives in the house?"

"Yes," answered Frank in embarrassed surprise.

"Do you know the party?"

"My mother once bore that name."

"All right! Here is the letter."

"Can it be from—him!" Frank asked himself in excitement.

He went up stairs hastily. His mother looked up in some surprise.

"Here is a letter for Mrs. Gerrish, mother; I thought I would bring it up at once."

"It must be from—him," said his mother changing color. "Where is it mailed?"

"Sing Sing," answered Frank briefly.

The letter was opened, and the two read it attentively. It ran thus:

MY DEAR WIFE:—I expect to leave this miserable place in a day or two, and hope you will be ready to welcome the returning prodigal. The five years I have spent here have seemed like twenty. It isn't the sort of a boarding house I would choose if I had liberty of choice. I long to be restored to your charming society, and doubtless the meeting will yield you equal satisfaction.

I don't know how you have got along as you haven't favored me with many letters of late. I suppose Frank has got to be quite a large boy, and brings you in quite a good sum every week. He will now have a father as well as mother to work for. We will make a cozy little family—the three of us. I quite yearn for domestic happiness, as I have been so long a stranger to it. Hoping to see you soon, I remain,

Your husband,
LUKE GERRISH.

Mother and son looked at each other in silent dismay, when they had read the letter.

"It is terrible!" murmured the former, pale and agitated. "We have been so happy by ourselves, and now——"

"Mother," said Frank firmly, "let us have nothing to do with this man!"

"Can we help it, Frank?"

"I don't know, but we will try."

"Do you remember him?"

"Yes; you know I was eleven when he was sent to prison. I remember what a relief it was to have him out of the way. It was a lucky thing for us when he committed the burglary that sent him to Sing Sing. What on earth could have induced you to marry him?"

"I married him for a home, knowing little about him. He represented himself as a man of means, in the real estate business, and I knew nothing of his intemperate habits. That he had any connection with housebreakers I was entirely ignorant, and the discovery was a great shock to me."

"How long did you live together before his arrest and imprisonment?"

"Two years—two unhappy years."

"When does he say he will be out?"

"In a day or two, and the letter is dated day before yesterday. He may be here any moment," she continued in visible agitation.

As she spoke a heavy step was heard ascending the stairs. Mother and son eyed each other apprehensively. The same thought was in the mind of both.

CHAPTER III.

LUKE GERRISH.

The steps halted before the door, and the latch was lifted. A man of large frame, with reddish hair and prominent features, with a pair of eyes abnormally small, shambled in, and peered curiously about him.

"Aha Mrs. G.," he said. "Glad to see you. It's long since we met. Shake hands."

Mrs. Manton, for she had resumed the name of her first husband, suffered him to take her hand, which he shook briefly, and then dropped.

"Haven't you anything to say to me, old lady?" he asked, gruffly.

"I hope you are well," she responded, but without any heartiness.

"Well?" he repeated. "How could you expect me to be well, after coming from such a place? No, I'm not well. I need to be soothed and cared for by a lovely woman, eh, my dear?"

Mrs. Manton looked uncomfortable. How, she asked herself, could she ever have married such a boor?

The eyes of Luke Gerrish wandered to Frank, who was surveying his stepfather with hardly repressed disgust.

"So this is the kid?" he said. "Shake hands, boy!"

He held out his hand, which Frank affected not to see.

"Sullen, eh?" muttered Gerrish, his small eyes contracting angrily. "What's your name?"

"Frank."

"Yes, I remember. Are you working?"

"Yes."

"How much do you earn?"

"Four dollars a week."

"Good! That's better than nothing. Have you got your last week's wages with you?"

"No."

"Where's your manners? Say no, sir."

"No, sir, if that suits you better."

"Look here, kid," said Gerrish, frowning ominously, "you ain't over polite to your father!"

"My father is dead, Mr. Gerrish."

"I'm your father now, and I mean that you shall treat me as such. When do you get your pay?"

"Saturday night."

"Good! You'll hand it to me every week. Do you hear?"

"Yes, I hear."

"Have you had supper, Mrs. G.?"

"Yes."

"Well, get some more, then. I am hungry."

"I have a little cold meat in the house, and can make you some tea and toast."

"Tea and toast! Bah! What do you take me for?"

"I think, Mr. Gerrish, as it is late, it will be better to get some supper at a restaurant," suggested Frank.

"I'm agreeable, if you'll supply the money."

"Here is a quarter," said Frank, producing a coin from his vest pocket.

"That isn't enough. What can I get for twenty five cents?"

"I have no more."

"Then I must apply to my better half. Mrs. G., if you'll give me another quarter, I will try to make it do."

She could hardly spare it, for rent day was near, but she felt that it was worth any sacrifice to get rid of this man. She produced another quarter, and he left the house.

Left alone, mother and son regarded each other with dismay.

"What can we do?" asked Mrs. Manton, sadly.

"I don't know, mother. I wish I did."

"This is only the beginning. He will be calling for money every day."

"Until he gets into trouble, and has to go back again."

"But in the meantime how can you get along? We shall not be able to meet the rent if we have to supply him with any more money."

"Then we won't!" said Frank, firmly. "If he finds there is no money to be had, he will go away."

"But he will force from me all the money I have."

"Give it to me, mother. He won't get it from me."

"But this will expose you to his fury."

"No; he won't know I have it. It will be the best way."

Mrs. Manton went to her drawer and brought out five dollars and a half, which she handed to Frank.

"Our rent is seven dollars," she said. "The dollar and a half which Mrs. Bond owes me will just meet the balance."

"Shall I take the work now?"

"Yes; perhaps it will be best."

"But suppose Mr. Gerrish comes back?"

"He will stay away the whole evening. He always used to."

Frank went to Forty Ninth Street, delivered the work, and received payment for it. This he added to the sum his mother had given him, and proceeded homeward. On the way he passed the office of the agent to whom the rent was usually paid. An idea struck him, and he entered the office.

"Good evening, Mr. Duncan," he said.

Duncan, a pleasant faced Scotchman, looked up.

"Ah, Frank," he said, "you haven't come to pay the rent before the time, have you?"

"Yes, I have, at least part of it, and I'll tell you why."

Thereupon he told Duncan about the unwelcome return of his stepfather.

"Eh, lad, you're in hard luck," said the friendly agent. "What can I do for you?"

"I want to pay you five dollars on account. Then Mr. Gerrish can't get hold of it, and we shall be owing you only two."

"A good idea, lad! Here, I'll give you a receipt on account. It's not many of my tenants pay me so long ahead of time. If your stepfather makes any fuss, send him to me."

"I will, if you don't mind, but he may make things unpleasant for you."

"If he does, he'll find things mighty unpleasant for him," said the agent, grimly.

"He's a strong man, Mr. Duncan."

"Come here, lad, and feel of that muscle," said the Scotchman.

Frank approached, and felt of the upper portion of the agent's arm. It was as hard as iron.

"There, what do you think of that?"

"I think you had better challenge John L. Sullivan. Where did you get so much muscle, Mr. Duncan?"

"We Scotchmen are fond of athletic sports. You ought to see me throw the hammer. I shall be ready to meet your respected stepfather if he likes to come round. Tell him so with my compliments."

"I will, as you don't mind."

When Frank went home he told his mother what he had done.

"You did right, Frank," she said. "That money, at least, is safe from Mr. Gerrish."

"I have two dollars left, mother."

"Perhaps it will be well to go out and buy some groceries, as he may get the money away during the night."

"A good idea, mother."

Frank went to a neighboring grocery store about an hour later, and bought some butter, sugar, and eggs. These he put into an empty basket which he had taken with him.

On his return home he walked along Seventh Avenue, which then, as now, possessed an unenviable notoriety as the promenade of gangs of ruffianly men and boys, whose delight it is to attack and rob peaceable wayfarers. Not since his earlier days had Frank been molested, but tonight was to prove an exception.

He had just crossed Thirty Sixth Street when two hoodlums, each a little larger than himself, halted in front of him.

"Say, kid, what have you got there?" asked the first.

"What business is it of yours?" demanded Frank.

"Say, cully, you're too fresh! Isn't he, Dick?"

"I should smile," answered the boy addressed as Dick.

"There's butter and eggs," said the first boy, peering into the basket. "That's just what me mother wants for our breakfast tomorrer. Kid, give me that basket."

"So you're thieves, are you?"

"Say that again, and I'll mash you! You must drop your basket right there, and maybe we won't hurt you."

As he spoke he grabbed the basket, and his companion was about to assist, when Frank, feeling that there was need for immediate action if he would save his purchases, snatched an egg from the basket and fired it full in the face of his first assailant. Of course the egg broke, and bespattered the face and eyes of the young ruffian, who drew back with an imprecation to wipe his face. Frank seized another egg and treated the second hoodlum in the same manner. While the two were wiping their nearly blinded eyes, he snatched up the basket and ran home, arriving safe with the loss of only two eggs.

CHAPTER IV.

AN UNPLEASANT INTERVIEW.

To the relief of the little household Luke Gerrish did not make his appearance again that evening. With the fifty cents in his possession he had betaken himself, not to a restaurant, but to a drinking saloon where he had been well acquainted in former days, and drank beer and whisky to the extent of his capital, satisfying his appetite with the free lunch always provided for patrons.

The result of his indulgence was, that at the end of the evening he was too stupid and drowsy to go home. The saloon keeper, who was an old acquaintance, made an exception in his favor, and bundled him into a small inner room, where on an old straw mattress on the floor he slept till late the next morning.

After breakfast on the following day Frank went to the store, and was soon engaged in his usual routine of duty. From twelve to one was his dinner hour. He usually went round to a small cheap restaurant. At one of the tables here sat his new acquaintance of the previous afternoon—Mr. John Carter.

Carter was the first to recognize him.

"Hallo, kid," he said, "come and sit down here."

Frank was curious to learn the contents of Carter's letter, and accepted the invitation.

"Did you get your letter?" he asked.

"Yes," answered Carter, shrugging his shoulders, "I got my letter, and much good it will do me."

"Wasn't it satisfactory?"

"You can read it and judge for yourself."

He drew the letter from his inside coat pocket and handed it to the office boy, who unfolded it and read as follows:

MR. JOHN CARTER:

I have received your letter, and wonder at your assurance in writing to ask assistance from me. You have wrecked your prospects, which were excellent, by your bad conduct and deserve no pity or help from any one. At the age of twenty one you received a bequest of thirty thousand dollars. This, if carefully husbanded, would have made you comfortable for life. How you squandered it you know better than any one else. I know that you drank and gambled; and shortened the life of your poor mother. Then, when you found yourself penniless, you forged a note on me for five hundred dollars, which for family reasons I hushed up and paid.

What your course of life has been since I don't know, but can easily conjecture. You have forfeited all claim upon me, and I hope I may never see you again. I inclose five dollars, not because you deserve it, but as a parting gift. It will be the last money you will ever receive from me, and this, I hope, will be my last communication.

SILAS SNOBDEN.

"That is a nice letter to receive, isn't it, kid?"

"Is all that your uncle says true?" asked Frank.

"About my legacy? Yes."

"And did you spend it as he says you did?"

"Part of it, but I made some bad investments. I was foolish, I dare say, but all business men have losses, don't they?"

"I dare say."

"Of course they do. I was unlucky—that's the whole of it."

"I should be glad if I could step into thirty thousand dollars at twenty one years of age."

"You'd lose it like me."

"I don't believe I should."

"You think yourself pretty smart, kid," sneered Carter.

Frank smiled.

"No, I don't," he said, "only prudent. I don't drink or gamble."

"Nor I—any longer. I tell you it's blamed mean to bring up all those old scores against me. Uncle Silas thinks thirty thousand dollars ought to have lasted me all my life."

"How much was your uncle worth when he was twenty one?"

"A few hundred dollars perhaps."

"Then he didn't inherit a fortune?"

"No."

"Yet now he is rich."

"He wouldn't be if he wasn't so plaguy mean. Why he could put his hand in his pocket and give me five thousand dollars without feeling it."

"Suppose he should, how long would it last you, Mr. Carter?" asked Frank.

"Look here, kid, I don't want you to lecture me. Wait till your beard grows. Boys of your age are apt to think they know more than old experienced men of the world. Why, I've forgotten more than you will ever know. Did you say my uncle generally stayed in his office after the store was closed up?"

"Yes."

"Say from five to six?"

"Yes."

"I shall have to call on him and have a little talk. I'll lay his duty before him, and make him ashamed of his meanness to a poor relation that's out of luck."

"I hardly think it will be any good. Mr. Snobden doesn't like to be interrupted when he is in his office."

"I'll take the risk of that," said Carter, carelessly. "There isn't much love lost between us at present. But I'm through breakfast and must be going. So long!"

He took the check beside his plate, and going up to the clerk paid for his breakfast and went out.

After he was fairly out of sight Frank noticed that he had left the letter on the table.

"I may as well take care of it," said the office boy, "and I can give it back to him when we meet."

The same day an unpleasant incident happened. One of the oldest men in the employ of Mr. Snobden was a certain man named Gideon Chapin. He had a son of about Frank's age whom he was anxious to get into the establishment. As there was no vacancy, it occurred to him that if he could get Frank discharged, a vacancy would be created. He was a sly, crafty man, who was not above misrepresentation if it would accomplish his purpose. During Frank's absence on an errand, he sought Mr. Snobden in his office.

"Mr. Snobden," he said, smoothly, "have you implicit confidence in your office boy?"

"I have implicit confidence in no one. Have you anything to tell me?"

"I—it is an unpleasant task—but I think I ought to tell you what I know."

"Of course you ought. Go on!"

"Last evening, then, I saw the office boy walking down Broadway in the company of a suspicious looking man."

"Indeed! Where did they go?"

"They went into the post office together. Was there any money in the letters which the boy Frank carried?"

"Yes, in one of them."

"I submit that valuable letters are hardly safe in the hands of a boy having disreputable acquaintances."

"Quite true. I will speak to Frank about it. Ah, here he is!"

As Frank entered the office he saw both men standing, but, as Mr. Chapin had frequent occasion to consult his employer, it didn't occur to him that he had anything to do with the interview till Mr. Snobden, pointing to him, said: "Is this the boy you saw last evening in disreputable company?"

"Yes; I can't be mistaken in a boy I see every day."

"Where was it, Mr. Chapin?" asked Frank, showing no trepidation.

"On the way to the post office, and in the post office."

"What have you to say?" asked Snobden, sternly.

"That it is true."

"So! the boy confesses!" said Chapin, triumphantly.

"Who was your companion?"

"It was your nephew, John Carter," answered Frank, quietly.

Mr. Snobden looked surprised.

"What did he want of you?"

"To ask about you. I told him I was about to mail a letter addressed to him, and he wished me to give it to him at once."

"Did you do so?" asked Snobden, quickly.

"No, I told him I had no authority to do so."

"Right!"

"Still he kept with me till he saw the letter deposited in the slit."

"I see nothing wrong in that, Mr. Chapin," said the merchant.

"N—no," said Chapin, with an air of discomfiture. "It *seems* satisfactory. I—I am really glad of it."

But as he left the office, Frank, observing his expression, knew that Mr. Chapin was his enemy, and that it behooved him to be on his guard against him.

That evening, as Silas Snobden sat in his office, the store door opened cautiously, and John Carter entered.

He looked around him, but saw no one. All the clerks had

been dismissed, and in the large establishment only the senior partner remained.

"The coast is clear—all the better!" he soliloquized. "I'll make a call on the old man, and see if I can work on his feelings, if he has any."

He made his way to the office, and entered unbidden.

Silas Snobden looked up, and a heavy frown gathered on his brow, when he recognized the intruder.

"How dare you come here?" he asked angrily. "Didn't you receive my letter?"

"Yes, Uncle Silas, I received it."

"I wrote you that I never wanted to see you again."

"Yes, it was a cold, hard, unfeeling letter," whined Carter. The merchant laughed scornfully.

"Do you mean to say you didn't deserve it?" he said.

"I know I haven't always been a model young man," whined Carter. "I have made mistakes, I admit, but all young men do that."

"Some make nothing but mistakes," said Mr. Snobden sharply. "Was the forged note a mistake?"

"I was mad—insane when I forged your signature."

His uncle eyed him sardonically.

"That's a very flimsy excuse. If you were insane then, I don't think you are too sane to make the same mistake again."

"Indeed. Uncle Silas, you do me injustice. I am a reformed man."

"You probably take me for a fool. I should be one if I put the least confidence in your word. Are you at work?"

"No; I am without work and without money."

"Probably you care little about obtaining work."

"That's where you are mistaken. I have a plan, if I were only able to carry it out."

"If it is a plan for working that is something new."

"I'll tell you what it is. There is a small cigar store on Third

Avenue that can be bought out for five hundred dollars. If I could only secure that I could support myself comfortably, and would never need to ask assistance again."

"When you have the money, you can try the experiment. In my opinion you would collapse in three months."

"Only try me, uncle. Give me a chance."

"What do you mean by that?"

"I mean that if you will lend me the money I will pay it back by monthly instalments. I think I can pay back the whole in a year. Such a sum as that would be a godsend to me. I will pay you any rate of interest."

"The investment is very tempting," said Mr. Snobden sarcastically, "but I shall have to decline."

"You won't give it to me?"

"No; I must request you leave me. My time is valuable," and Mr. Snobden turned to resume his work.

John Carter rose slowly to his feet. Beside his uncle on the desk was a roll of bills, which he had just been counting, and an office ruler. With a quick movement he dashed forward, seized the money, and on his uncle grasping him dealt him a blow on the head with the ruler, which stretched him senseless on the floor. Then he made good his escape from the store and hurried from the vicinity.

Five minutes later Frank, who had again been sent on an errand after hours, entered the office, and was horror struck when he saw his employer lying on the floor, his face pale as ashes and covered with blood.

As he was bending over the prostrate form, a policeman, who, in going his rounds, had caught sight through the front window of the stricken man, entered and placed a heavy hand on Frank's shoulder.

"Boy," he said, "you are my prisoner!"

CHAPTER V.

FRANK'S VINDICATION.

Frank looked up and eyed the policeman in amazement.

"What do you mean?" he asked.

"You know well enough what I mean, you young rascal! I've caught you in the act."

"In what act?"

"Murderin' and robbin' your employer! You'll swing on the gallers yet, you young villain!"

Frank hardly knew whether to be most amused or indignant. He could not realize that the officer was in earnest, but when he found his hands incased in handcuffs, he decided that he was in serious trouble.

"Listen!" he said. "I only just returned from an errand, and, entering the office to report to Mr. Snobden, I found him lying senseless on the floor."

"That's too thin! You don't fool me so easy."

"How could I—a boy—strike down a man like Mr. Snobden?"

"I've heard of a boy murderer who only weighed seventy three pounds. You're a stout, strong boy, and you probably crept up behind the old man and gave him a blow with that ruler."

"You must be crazy!"

"None of your impudence, boy! I shall take you along to the station house as soon as I can get help for the old man. Come with me while I rap for assistance."

He forced Frank to accompany him to the sidewalk, and

rapped for help. Two other officers appeared on the scene, and together they went back to the office.

"What has the boy done?" asked officer Snow of the first policeman.

"Tried to murder his employer," answered the other gruffly.

Snow looked scrutinizingly at Frank. He had a kindly, benevolent face, and had a boy at home about Frank's age.

"Did you see him do it?" he asked.

"I saw him bendin' over the old man just after it happened."

"So you concluded he did it? Boy, how long had you been in the office?"

"Just got in. I had been on an errand."

"Do you know of any one being with Mr. Snobden?"

"There was no one with him when I went out."

"You see," said the first policeman, "I understand my business, I do."

"No offense to you, Grubb, but if this boy isn't the one who attacked Mr. Snobden, we must find the man that did."

"If Mr. Snobden would only come to, he would tell you," said Frank.

"A good suggestion. Is there any water in the building? Perhaps we can bring him to."

"Yes, I'll go for some," and then Frank stopped short, for, with his hands confined by handcuffs, he was helpless.

"Unfasten the handcuffs, Grubb. Surely you are not afraid the boy will prove too much for you?"

"If he escapes, you will be to blame," said Grubb, reluctantly complying with the directions of officer Snow, who, he knew, was a man of influence at headquarters.

Frank returned with a pail of water, which officer Snow took from him, and bathed the face of the prostrate man. It had the desired effect, for he shivered slightly, and opened his eyes.

"Where am I?" he asked, wildly. "What has happened?"

"You have been struck down. We found you on the floor. Can

you tell us who attacked you? Was it this boy?" pointing to Frank.

"No—no," answered Snobden.

"Who was it, then?"

"Help me up! Let me think!" and he put his hand to his head with an air of doubt.

Officer Snow eyed Grubb with a glance of triumph.

"What did I tell you?" he said. "The boy is innocent, as I said."

"I don't know about that. The old man is dazed."

Meanwhile Mr. Snobden was trying to collect his thoughts.

"Who was with you—whom do you remember seeing last?" added Snow.

The old man's face cleared up.

"I know—I know," he murmured. "It was John Carter, my rascally nephew. It was he that struck me."

"Do you know this Carter, my boy?" asked officer Snow, addressing Frank.

"Yes," answered Frank, with a look of sudden comprehension. "I met him today in a restaurant. He asked me if his uncle remained in the office after hours, and I told him that he generally stayed here till six o'clock."

"It is now twenty minutes of six," said officer Snow, consulting his watch.

"Do you know if there was any disagreement—any quarrel between John Carter and his uncle?"

"Yes; he had written to his uncle for money, and received in return a severe letter."

"Evidently we must look for Carter," said officer Snow.

"I don't believe there is any such man," said officer Grubb, stubbornly.

Snow said nothing, but gave him a look of contempt.

"Did your nephew steal anything?" he asked of Snobden.

"Yes; he seized a pile of bills I had on the desk beside me."

"Do you know the amount of money taken?"

"One hundred and twenty one dollars. I had just counted it."

"Did you and your nephew have a quarrel?"

"Yes; he asked me for money, and I refused."

"And then he attacked you?"

"Yes; he took me by surprise. If I had had any warning of his intention I would have resisted. Am I much hurt?" he asked, anxiously, putting his hand to his head, and shuddering a little as he saw the blood upon his fingers.

Officer Snow examined the part of the head on which the blow had fallen.

"I am a little of a surgeon," he said, "and can assure you that it is nothing serious. You had better ride home. Your boy here can call a cab."

"Yes, Frank," said the merchant. "You may go out and call a carriage."

"Give me your handkerchief, and I will bind up the wound," said Snow. "Do you wish your nephew arrested?"

"Yes," answered Snobden, vindictively. "Arrest him! Don't let him escape! I will appear against him."

"Do you know where he lives?"

"I have a letter from him somewhere, but I don't know where it is. Wait till the boy returns; he may remember."

Frank came back in a very short time with a carriage, and helped Mr. Snobden into it.

"I hope you are not much hurt, sir," he said.

"I am not going to die this time, I think," said Snobden, grimly, "but I mean to make my graceless nephew suffer for what he has done. Do you remember the address of the letter which I sent him?"

"Yes, sir: No. 17 1-2 East Fourth St."

"Yes, yes, that's it," said Snobden, eagerly. "Go with the officers and point him out. I want him arrested. It will take up your time, but you won't lose anything by it. Here—here is a dollar."

"Thank you, sir."

"You are a good boy. I'll raise your wages, after all. You shall have five dollars instead of four."

"Thank you, sir," said Frank, gladly. "It will be a great help to me."

"What do you think now, Grubb?" asked officer Snow. "This is the boy you were so sure had tried to murder the old man. Now his employer raises his pay."

"I don't take any stock in the boy," said Grubb, sullenly. "Old Snobden doesn't know who attacked him. It may have been the boy, after all."

Officer Snow turned from him with a look of disgust.

"I see you are bound to have the boy guilty. You are what I call a fair minded man. You would hound an innocent man to prison rather than admit that you were wrong."

"I don't like that talk. I am an officer as well as you."

"That is true."

"And I've got just as much right to my opinion as you."

"Oh, you can think as you please, so long as you don't act unjustly. Come, my boy, we will go in search of this man Carter."

CHAPTER VI.

TWO BOON COMPANIONS.

When John Carter had dealt his uncle that cowardly blow and snatched the roll of bills he lost no time in escaping from the store. He hurried along White Street to Broadway, walked up to the St. Charles Hotel, and entering, ordered a substantial meal, which he paid for out of the stolen money.

He seized the opportunity, while waiting, to count the bills.

"One hundred and twenty one dollars!" he soliloquized complacently. "That's a godsend. It will keep me from starving for a time. I wonder how hard I hit the old man. I shouldn't care much if the blow finished him, only it might get me into trouble. I suppose it's too much to expect that I am down in the old fellow's will."

Carter ate his meal with great relish. He had a good appetite, not having eaten anything since breakfast. The thought of what he had done did not trouble him at all, for his conscience was not sensitive.

He had nearly finished his repast when a gentleman with whom we are already acquainted—Luke Gerrish—entered. He had not yet returned to the home of Mrs. Manton, but was looking up old acquaintances. He had heard that one was staying at the St. Charles Hotel, but had found him absent. Having ten cents, which he had borrowed from the saloon keeper, he went into the restaurant to buy as much food as it would command. His face lighted up when he recognized John Carter.

"Can I believe my eyes—Jack!" he ejaculated, hurrying forward with extended hand.

"O, it's you, Luke!" said Carter. "Where do you come from?"

Gerrish jerked his thumb significantly in the direction of his home for the last five years. The motion was understood, for Carter had been one of his fellow boarders, though not for so long a time.

Luke Gerrish eyed the oyster pie which Carter was eating with a hungry look.

"I say, Jack, you seem to be in funds," he said.

"Yes, slightly. Will you dine with me?"

"Will I? Well I should smile. I've had nothing to eat today."

"Give your order, then."

"Waiter, an oyster pie, and coffee, and be quick about it. I'm famished."

"You've got a wife in the city, haven't you? I think you told me so."

"Yes."

"Have you been to see her?"

"Yes; but she didn't seem very glad to see me. Gave me the cold shake, in fact! Think of a wife like that!"

"Well, Gerrish, you ain't exactly the man to inspire devoted affection. Are you living at home?"

"No, but I mean to. The old lady and her boy ain't goin' to turn me out into the streets if I know it."

"Good for you! So there's a boy, is there?"

"Yes, but not mine. You see I married a widow."

"She married you for your money, or was it your beauty?"

"A little of both," answered Gerrish with a grin. "She thought I had money, and would support her and the kid."

"How old is the boy?"

"About sixteen."

"What's his name?"

"Frank Manton."

"Seems to me I have heard that name before. Is he working?"

"Yes, he's working in a mercantile house down town—firm of Snobden & Downs."

"You don't mean it!" exclaimed Carter, in some excitement.

"Why shouldn't I mean it? Is there anything strange about his working for that firm?"

"Perhaps you don't know that Silas Snobden's my uncle."

Luke Gerrish, with his cup half way to his mouth, stopped short and stared at his companion in astonishment.

"Silas Snobden your uncle?" he repeated.

"Yes."

"Then you're in luck. He must be very rich."

"Much good his money does me."

"Aren't you friends?"

"He treats me like a dog!" said John Carter, vehemently. "Why, he's rolling in wealth, and he wouldn't give me a dollar to save me from starving."

"You've got some money, haven't you?"

"Yes, a little," was the guarded reply.

"How did you get that?"

"By a lucky speculation. It isn't much, but I can stand your dinner. So go ahead, and eat as much as you like."

"Thank you, Jack. You're a good sort after all."

"When did you get out?"

"I've been out only a day or two."

"What are you going to do?"

"The boy's got to help support me. Do you know how much your uncle pays him?"

"How should I know? I've met the boy, and he's an impudent young cub—impudent and disobliging. Excuse my saying so."

"O, go ahead! Say what you like about him. You won't hurt my feelings. I ain't very fond of the kid myself. Why, he ain't respectful to me. Think of that—and me his father!"

"I had a little adventure with him myself, Luke. I hope you'll teach him a good lesson."

"I will—trust me for that! I'm goin' to collect his pay myself after this. What's the number of your uncle's store?"

Carter gave it.

"All right! I'll call and see the old gentleman. Shall I give him your love?"

John Carter looked queer. Before him rose the picture of that senseless and prostrate form, and he felt a little uncomfortable.

"No, don't say anything about me," he replied hastily. "I don't expect to have anything to do with my uncle. He's down on me."

Luke Gerrish had by this time finished the oyster pie, but he still felt hungry.

"Have some pudding, old man?"

"No; if you don't mind I'll take another oyster pie."

"All right! It's all the same to me."

Ten minutes later the second pie was dispatched, and the two rose from the table. John Carter drew out a five dollar bill from the roll, and paid the two checks.

"Where are you goin'?" asked Gerrish, who thought it worth while to keep in with a man who seemed in such good luck.

"I'm going round to my room, 17 1-2 East Fourth Street. Will you come? It's only a little way."

"Yes, I'll come. Are you goin' to stay in the city?"

"I am not sure."

"Suppose my uncle recovers and reports that I attacked and robbed him?" This was the thought that suddenly flashed upon Carter. "He knows where I room, and can put the police on my track. I must move without delay, and it will be better to leave the city. I will go to Philadelphia tomorrow morning, and stay till I hear how things are coming out."

This was a very prudent resolution on the part of John Carter, but he did not appreciate the importance of carrying out his plan without delay. He did not know that the police, accompanied by Frank Manton, were already on their way to his room on East Fourth Street.

The two turned down a street leading to the Bowery, and walked in leisurely fashion to East Fourth Street. They stopped at a drinking saloon, and Carter stood treat.

"I'm glad I met you, Jack," said Gerrish. "I never thought you were such a good fellow before."

"I wish my uncle had as good an opinion of me as you have."

"Maybe the old hunks will come round."

"Not much! He's got a heart as hard as a millstone."

Meanwhile, such had been the delay at the restaurant, that Frank and the two officers (Grubb and Snow) had reached Carter's lodgings already.

"Go up and inquire for the party, my boy," said officer Snow. "We will keep in the background."

Frank rang the bell of a three story brick house.

The summons was answered by a slatternly looking woman, who seemed to have come up from the kitchen.

"Does Mr. Carter live here?" asked Frank politely.

"Yes, he's the man on the third floor back. If you're a friend of his, I wish you would tell him to pay his rent."

"Is he owing you money?"

"He's owing me four dollars, and I'm a lone widder, and can't stand the loss."

"I will speak to him about it. Do you know if he's in his room?"

"You can go up and see. I've got too much to do to keep watch of my lodgers."

"Thank you! I will go up and see if he's in."

Frank ascended the stairs, knocked at the door of Carter's room, but, hearing no answer, opened it and looked in.

CHAPTER VII.

CARTER PLAYS A TRICK ON GERRISH.

The room was empty, and beyond a small carpet bag, and a brush and comb on the bureau, there was nothing to indicate that it was occupied.

"He doesn't appear to have come in," said Frank to himself. "What shall I do?"

He decided to remain in the room for five minutes at least, in the hope of seeing the man he was after. His hope was realized, for within that time he heard footsteps on the stairs, and soon saw the door open and two men enter, one the occupant of the room, the other Luke Gerrish.

Now there was no one whom he less expected to see than his stepfather, and the same may be said of Gerrish. He was far from expecting to see his stepson.

"Why it's the kid!" he exclaimed, turning to Carter.

"Is that your stepson? He is also an acquaintance of mine," said Carter. "What are you here for?" he asked, not without anxiety, for he was afraid suspicion might have fallen upon him.

This was a question which for the moment nonplused Frank. He knew very well what was the object of his errand, but this of course he could not reveal to Carter. Fortunately he was quick witted, and this fact suggested a reply which would not excite John Carter's suspicion.

"I think you told me that you are the nephew of Mr. Silas Snobden?" he said.

"Certainly," answered Carter cautiously.

"Then it is only right for me to tell you as a near relative that your uncle has met with a bad accident."

"You don't tell me so?" ejaculated Carter with well counterfeited surprise.

"Out with it, kid!" said Gerrish, to whom of course Carter had said nothing about the matter.

"When I returned to the office about half past five o'clock I found him lying on his back on the floor of the office."

"Is it possible?" asked Carter. "Was it an apoplectic stroke?"

"No; he had been knocked down, and robbed of some bills which lay on the desk beside him."

"You don't mean it! Who could have done it?"

"I can't tell."

"Probably it was some clerk who knew that he was in the habit of staying behind after the store was closed."

"I can't think of any one of the clerks who would do such a thing."

"I've lived in the world longer than you, and I feel sure that was the way it happened," said Carter positively.

"You may be right," answered Frank noncommittally.

"I'm very much obliged to you for coming to tell me about it."

"In case Mr. Snobden dies you may be his heir," suggested Frank slyly.

"To be sure!" returned Carter, as a new and joyful prospect was unfolded to him by these words. "He has no sons, and I think it probable I would inherit something. But I hope there is no chance of his dying?"

"I hope not too. Would you like to go back with me and see him?"

"Thank you," answered Carter quickly. "I shall not be able to go at once, but I may call tomorrow morning. What was done with him?"

"He was carried home in a hack."

"Quite right. It was what I would have advised."

"Having delivered my message, I won't stay any longer, Mr. Carter. I hope you won't think me officious for coming."

"Not at all, not at all! I am very much obliged to you."

Frank was about to leave the room when Luke Gerrish called him back.

"Look here, boy," he said, "tell your mother that I shall probably be home this evening."

"I will tell her," answered Frank, coldly.

"I stopped with a friend last night—one whom I had not seen for some time."

Frank nodded.

"And hark you, kid, you must pay your next salary to me. Do you hear?"

"I hear you, sir."

"You'd better remember, too. I have as much right to it as your mother."

"I hear you, sir."

"That is well. If you behave right you will find me a kind and indulgent parent, but if you rile me, you'll wish you hadn't, that's all."

Frank retired without making an attempt to answer and reported to the policemen below that their man was up stairs.

He then went home at once. On entering his mother's room, he found her with a letter in her hand.

"Read that, Frank," she said. "It is from your Uncle George, who left home when he was a mere boy. We all thought him dead, but he is alive, and living in Southern California."

"Does he say how he is situated?" asked Frank.

"No; but he says he may soon come East."

"How did he know your address?"

"He met an early friend, Mr. Manning, who gave him the information."

Frank read the letter, and then acquainted his mother with the attack on his employer.

After he had left the room Luke Gerrish turned to Carter with a significant smile.

"Now I know where you got your money," he said.

"What do you mean?" asked Carter, flushing up.

"I mean that you are the one who attacked your uncle in his office and then robbed him."

"You have no right to say so. You know nothing about it," blustered Carter.

"Look here, Jack, that don't go down with me. I know you too well. You'll be in a scrape if Mr. Snobden dies."

"Pooh! I don't believe there is any danger of it."

"You ought to know. You know what sort of a blow you dealt him."

"I don't want you to talk in that way, Luke Gerrish," said Carter, angrily.

"How much money did you get?"

"Oh, rubbish! What business is it of yours?"

"It may be my business, if you don't share with me. I'm awfully hard up. Give me twenty dollars."

"Well, I like your impudence. I won't give you a cent."

"You won't? Then I'll go and tell Mr. Snobden that you are the one who attacked him."

"Go ahead and tell him so. I am perfectly willing," answered Carter.

Luke Gerrish was rather taken aback by Carter's cool indifference. He began to think he was mistaken. It didn't occur to him that he would be only telling old news. It did occur to him, however, that the indifference might be only feigned, in order to get rid of paying him any money.

Carter had occasion to go out into the hall. There he met the landlady's son, a boy of twelve.

"Oh, Mr. Carter," he said, "what do you think? There is two policemen standing on the opposite side of the street, watching the house. What is it for, do you think?"

John Carter's heart gave a sudden thump. He understood it well enough.

"How should I know?" he inquired. "How long have they been there?"

"About fifteen minutes."

"I know what it means, then."

"What?" asked the boy, curiously.

"It is a secret," answered Carter, lightly. "I'll tell you what I want you to do. Go out in about ten minutes, and ask the policemen if they want any one in this house."

"Yes," replied the boy, with eyes like saucers.

"Or rather, go up stairs and tell the man you find there that I am waiting for him in the street."

"But will you be there?"

"Yes; now I want to go down stairs into the kitchen a minute."

"All right!" said the boy, looking puzzled.

John Carter went back into the room, and found Luke Gerrish looking a little uneasy.

"Where have you been?" he asked.

"Down stairs, to see about some washing I want done."

"Do they wash here?"

"Only for the people in the house. Then there's something I have forgotten. By the way, Luke, if you are short, I don't mind lending you a tenner. There it is!"

Luke took it, agreeably surprised, and disposed to think better of Carter than before.

"That's kind of you, Carter; I stand in need of it, for I haven't a cent."

"Oh, you're welcome, only don't imagine I got it from my uncle. I wish he would come down handsome, but I haven't much hope of it. Wait here a minute! I'll be back directly."

Carter put on his hat, went down stairs, passed into the back yard, no one being in the kitchen, got over the fence into a vacant lot, and vanished.

Up came Tommy, according to directions, and said to Gerrish, "Mr. Carter's waiting for you out in the street."

"All right!"

Luke Gerrish, unsuspecting, went down to the front door and out on the sidewalk.

While he was looking in every direction two policemen crossed the street.

"You must come with me, John Carter!" said officer Grubb, placing his hand on his shoulder.

"What do you mean?" asked Gerrish, trying to shake himself free from the officer's grasp.

"You're wanted!"

"Who do you take me for?"

The reader will recall that Frank, having fulfilled his duty as guide, and led the policemen to the residence of the man they were in search of, had returned to the Bowery, and taken a Fourth Avenue car up town.

"You are John Carter," said the officer.

Gerrish burst into an amused laugh.

"Am I?" he retorted. "Come, that's a good joke."

"You don't get off that way."

"I don't want to. But first tell me what I am accused of."

"Of attacking and robbing Mr. Silas Snobden."

"That's a likely story. I never saw the man in my life."

"Are you not his nephew?"

"No. If you doubt it, you can take me to him and ask him."

"Do you know where John Carter is?"

"He was in the house with me a few minutes since. He left the room, and sent word for me to join him on the sidewalk."

"I don't believe a word of it," said officer Grubb gruffly. "This man is John Carter, I make no doubt."

"Ring the bell," said Gerrish coolly, "and ask the landlady—I don't know her name—if I am John Carter."

"A good suggestion!" said officer Snow. And he rang the bell.

The landlady appeared. She looked surprised and alarmed when she saw the policeman.

"Is this man John Carter, a lodger of yours?" asked Grubb.

"Certainly not! I don't know the man."

Grubb looked crestfallen.

"Where is Carter, then?"

"I expect he's in his room. What has he been doing, gentlemen?"

"Robbery and murder, ma'am! That's all."

"Oh, my goodness gracious!" exclaimed Mrs. Stubbs, horror stricken, "and he so innercent lookin'. And he's lived under this ruff for a month. It's a mercy we ain't all been murdered in our beds."

"Will you go up and see if Carter is in his room, ma'am?"

"I can tell you he isn't," said Gerrish. "I didn't think he was so sly. He left me a few minutes since, and said he was going down stairs to see about his washing."

"He doesn't have any washing done here," interjected the landlady.

"It was a fake, then! It's my opinion he's got off by the way of the back yard."

"Let me go down stairs," said officer Snow. "You stay here, Grubb, in case he is really up stairs, and tries to make a bolt."

When Snow saw how easy it was to escape over the back fence, he thought it useless to ask any more questions.

"The bird's flown!" he reported, on his return.

"Gentlemen," said Luke Gerrish, "I'm sorry for your disappointment, though I admit Carter is an acquaintance of mine. But I never thought he was up to such a thing as robbery and murder. It shocks me, it does really!"

"I have no doubt of it," said Grubb with sarcasm. "You look like a pious man."

"Do I? You're very kind to say so, but I am afraid I don't deserve it, though I have been pretty regular in my attendance on religious services for some years."

He did not think it necessary to mention that his incarceration in Sing Sing accounted for the regularity.

"I suppose I may go now."

"Wait a minute!" said Grubb. "How do we know but you're Carter's confederate?"

"Oh, gentlemen, this is too much!"

"Is it? Snow, hadn't we better see if he has any of the stolen money?"

"Yes."

"You may search and welcome. All the money you will find is a ten dollar bill."

"Show it."

Gerrish drew out the bill which he had not yet had time to examine.

Grubb took it and scrutinized it.

"Aha! what is this?" he said, pointing to a red stain on one corner.

"*It is blood!*" said Snow, quietly. "You must come along with us."

Luke Gerrish turned pale. He was innocent, for a wonder, but he saw that this discovery would weigh heavily against him.

"The scoundrel!" he ejaculated. "He must have done this on purpose."

CHAPTER VIII.

THE TELLTALE NOTE.

"I mean that John Carter paid me this money only a short time since," Gerrish said to the officers, in explanation of his exclamation recorded at the close of the last chapter.

"In payment of a debt?"

"No," answered Gerrish, who was shrewd enough to see that it was wise in this instance to tell the truth. "I saw that he had a roll of bills and asked him to lend me something, as I was hard up."

"And he gave you this bill?"

"Yes."

"Have you any others?"

"No. You had better search me, and satisfy yourselves."

The officers did so, but discovered nothing else.

"Now will you let me go?"

"No. We shall need you as a witness even if you are not a confederate."

"I am a friend of Mr. Snobden," said Gerrish boldly.

"I thought you said you didn't know him."

"I don't, but my son is in his employ."

"Who is your son?"

"The boy who brought you here."

In the hurry of the moment Frank had not mentioned that the man with Carter was his stepfather, and this relation astonished the officers. They did not know whether to believe it or not.

"Then perhaps the boy was in the plot," suggested Grubb suspiciously.

"No, he wasn't. I ain't overfond of him, but he ain't one of that sort. Take me along, gentlemen! I'm willing to go. If I can help you about this matter, I will. Mr. Snobden is the employer of my son, and I wish him well. He won't die, will he?"

"No; his injuries do not appear to be serious, though your friend dealt him a powerful blow."

"Don't call that black hearted rascal my friend! I only hope you'll get hold of him."

"Have you any idea where he is likely to conceal himself?"

"No, I haven't, but I don't believe he'll stay in the city, or come back to his room. He has lived in Philadelphia."

"Then very likely he will go there. I will send an alarm to the Central Office."

It was finally decided to take Gerrish to the private residence of Mr. Snobden to see if that gentleman could identify him.

Luke made no opposition, but on the contrary expressed satisfaction when told that this was to be done.

"I'd like to meet the old gentleman," he said.

He was taken up into Mr. Snobden's bed chamber. The merchant, his head bandaged up, was lying back in an easy chair. He looked up as Gerrish was brought into his presence.

"Do you recognize this man, Mr. Snobden?" asked officer Snow.

The old man eyed the visitor keenly.

"No," he said slowly, "I don't think I ever saw him before."

"Then he is not the man who assaulted you?"

"Certainly not," answered the merchant sharply. "Didn't I tell you that it was my nephew—John Carter—who struck me?"

"This man is a friend of John Carter. He was found in his company."

"He might have been found in better company," said Silas Snobden grimly.

"And we found on his person this blood stained bill," continued Grubb.

Silas Snobden took it in his hand.

"It is one of the bills stolen from me," he said.

"How do you know?"

"It was drawn from the Park Bank today. I had occasion to use a sum of money, and this is one of the bills."

"Then you positively identify it?"

"I can't go as far as that, for there are a good many bills on the Park Bank. I have no doubt it was one of the bills taken from me."

"Excuse me for asking it back," said officer Snow as Snobden was about putting it in his pocket. "We must keep it as an important piece of evidence."

"Very well!"

Luke Gerrish was taken to the police station, but as Carter was still at large, and Mr. Snobden disclaimed all knowledge of him, he was allowed to go, much to his relief, but was not permitted to take with him the blood stained bill, greatly to his regret.

CHAPTER IX.
FRANK'S STEPFATHER.

Frank and his mother were spared one annoyance. Luke Gerrish, though he came to meals when he had nowhere else to go, did not attempt to make his home with them. A shady acquaintance of his had a residence near the North River on Fortieth Street, and he found this a home more congenial to his tastes. But of one thing he did not lose sight—his resolution to appropriate Frank's earnings to his own use. On Saturday morning he presented himself at the store of Snobden & Downs. He entered the establishment, and looked round him rather awkwardly, not feeling at home in such a place.

"What can I do for you, sir?" asked Charles Harmons, one of the clerks, eying him with some curiosity, for he hardly looked like a customer.

"Is Mr. Snobden here?" asked Gerrish.

"Yes; but he is engaged. Do you wish to see him on business?"

"Yes."

"You are sure you wish to see him on business? His time is valuable."

"So is mine," answered Gerrish, straightening up. "Young man, I wish you to distinctly understand that I want to see Snobden on business."

The clerk looked doubtful, but reflected that Gerrish might be a country customer, rich and eccentric, though he certainly did not look as if he were overburdened with money.

"Well, I'll ask him if he will see you," he said.

He went to the office, and returned almost immediately, saying, "Follow me."

Gerrish gave a twist to rather a disreputable cravat which had got out of place, and followed the clerk into the presence of Silas Snobden.

Mr. Snobden, whose head was still bandaged, looked up sharply as Luke Gerrish entered the office.

"Well, what do you want?" he asked.

"Perhaps you recognize me, Mr. Snobden," said Gerrish, coughing a little.

"Yes; you are the friend of my graceless nephew."

"I was, sir, I was, but never after this will Luke Gerrish be a friend to that scroundrel. After his base attack upon his kind benefactor——"

"I am not his kind benefactor—I never will be!" said Snobden sharply.

"And serve him right. I hope you will disinherit him."

"Do you know where he is?"

"No, sir."

"Then what business have you with me? My time is valuable."

"I have a son in your employ, Mr. Snobden—a son to whom you have been kind."

"His name?"

"Frank Manton."

"Is Frank Manton your son?" asked Silas Snobden in surprise.

"Yes, sir, my stepson. I hope you find him satisfactory."

"Well, I don't complain of him."

"He is a good boy, but of course he has his faults. I don't think boys of his age ought to be trusted with money. It may lead them into temptation, so I have called to say that I will call every week to receive his salary."

9. Gerrish found himself
on the sidewalk.

10. "Good evening, Frank. This is my little boy, Rob."

11. Gerrish was seized from behind.

12. The door was opened
by Benson's mother.

13. An unpleasant surprise for Frank Manton.

14. "Why do you keep watching me, Mr. Chapin?"

15. "I hear you've been bounced."

16. Seth Hastings seized Gerrish by the collar.

"Quite against our rules!" said Mr. Snobden. "We only pay to the parties in our employ."

"But, sir, he is a minor. I am his father and guardian."

"Are you? I am not sure of that. I will soon ascertain."

He rang the bell, and a clerk responded.

"Send Frank Manton here."

Frank, who was near at hand, received the summons, and soon presented himself. He looked at Gerrish with surprise.

"Frank, do you know this man?" asked Snobden.

"Yes, sir, I am sorry to say I do."

"Who is he?"

"My mother unfortunately married him some years since in ignorance of his character."

"You see, sir," said Gerrish, triumphantly, "the kid admits it."

"We have no kids here, sir," said Snobden stiffly.

"The boy, then."

"I hope, Mr. Snobden, he has not annoyed you."

"He asks me to pay your weekly salary to him, Frank."

"I hope you won't do it, sir. My mother needs all I can earn. He would only spend it on drink."

"Treat your father with more respect!" said Gerrish frowning.

"I treat you with all the respect you deserve, Mr. Gerrish."

"Why have you never mentioned that you had a stepfather before?" asked the merchant.

"I wanted to forget it."

"Why didn't you come up and call for the boy's wages before, Mr.—Gerrish?"

"I was absent from the city, sir," answered Luke Gerrish uneasily.

"At Sing Sing prison," added Frank, bluntly.

"Ha! I see. So you are a convict!"

"I was the victim of a conspiracy, sir. I solemnly swear to you that I was an innocent man. It was a great trial to me to associate with the bad men I met in the prison."

"Gerrish, I am of opinion that you met no men worse than yourself. I am sorry that my office boy is in any way connected with such a man. I certainly shall not pay his wages to any one else except himself or his mother."

"Thank you, Mr. Snobden," said Frank, feeling much relieved. "I hope you won't think any the worse of me for having such a stepfather."

"No, Frank," answered his employer not unkindly. "I don't think you will long be troubled with him. He will soon return to his home up the river in all probability."

"You are unjust, sir," said Gerrish with an attempt at dignity. "Rich men have hard hearts."

"And hard heads too, Gerrish! They don't allow themselves to be imposed upon by men of your stripe. You can go, sir."

"I don't think I ought to allow my son to remain with an employer who insults his father."

"I hope, Mr. Snobden, you won't pay any attention to what this man says."

"The only attention I shall pay to him is to order his ejection from the store unless he goes out at once of his own accord."

"You will be sorry for your treatment of me, Mr. Snobden. I know I am poor, but——"

"So was I once," retorted Snobden. "An honest poor man I can respect, but there is not an honest bone in your body. Now, sir, let me bid you good morning. I do not wish to receive another call from you."

Luke Gerrish had considerable assurance, but even he felt that he had no pretext for staying longer. Silas Snobden was a small, frail man, but there was a weight of authority in his words that Gerrish could not withstand.

"I'd like to be alone with him," he muttered to himself, as he left the counting room with considerably less words than when he entered it.

"Come out with me! I want to speak to you, kid," he said, with a final attempt to assert himself.

"My time belongs to Mr. Snobden," answered Frank, coolly turning his back upon his stepfather.

"I'll make it hot for you when you get home, you ungrateful kid."

"Tell John to see this man out," said the merchant.

John was a strong, able bodied porter, who was at work just outside the office.

Luke Gerrish stole a glance at him, and it occurred to him that he had better go out without his assistance.

He was considerably disappointed, for he had expected that Mr. Snobden would readily comply with his request, and Frank's pay would supply him with spending money.

"The boy's too much for me," he muttered, "but his mother must earn something and it will go hard with me if I don't get my share of it."

Mrs. Manton was not particularly pleased when her shiftless husband came upstairs and entered the room without knocking at the door.

"Good morning Mrs. G.," he said, sinking into the nearest chair. "I don't know but you thought I had deserted you."

"No, I didn't think that," answered Mrs. Manton dryly.

"Sewing, eh? I suppose you are pretty well paid for your work."

"If you consider twenty five cents a day good pay."

"Come, now, don't you get more than that? Honor bright!" persisted Gerrish.

"No; I wish I did."

"You'd better let me go round and ask your customers to pay you better. I will tell them you can't afford to work a whole day for such paltry compensation."

"It would do no good, Mr. Gerrish. I should lose them, that is all."

"I think, my dear, I must trouble you to let me have half a dollar," said Gerrish coughing. "I am quite penniless, I assure you I am."

"I have no money for you," said Mrs. Manton with a flash of indignation. "You will have to work as I do."

"I intend to, Mrs. G., and when I get well started I hope to support you in comfort. When does your rent come due?"

"On Saturday."

"Then you must have some money laid up for that purpose. Let me have some of it, and I'll return it to you."

"I can't oblige you. Frank paid five dollars on account a day or two since."

"Ah! I see! You don't want me to get hold of the money?" said Gerrish indignantly. "To whom is the rent payable?"

"To James Duncan, at his office in Sixth Avenue."

"All right! I'll go and see Mr. Duncan."

CHAPTER X.

LUKE GERRISH MAKES A CALL.

Mr. Duncan was sitting in his office with an account book before him, when Luke Gerrish swaggered in.

"Is your name Duncan?" he asked in a bullying tone.

"Yes, sir; what can I do for you?"

"My wife hires her room from you."

"Very well. What is your name?"

"Luke Gerrish."

"There is no Mrs. Gerrish among my tenants."

"She calls herself Manton. She seems to think that is a prettier name than Gerrish, but Mrs. Gerrish she is all the same."

"So this is Frank's stepfather," thought Duncan. "He looks like a bully."

"Mrs. Manton hires from me," he said quietly.

"My boy came over the other day and paid you some rent ahead of time."

"Yes; he paid me five dollars on account of next month's rent."

"He did so without my authority. I have occasion for that money. You may return it to me, and you will be paid when the first of the month comes."

"Pardon me, sir, but I don't know you in this matter."

"Do you doubt my word?" blustered Gerrish.

"Really, my dear sir, I won't express any opinion upon that point. If now you had brought a letter from Mrs. Manton, or Mrs. Gerrish, as you call her, that would simplify matters."

"Is not my word as good as hers?"

"It may be. I hope it is, but you are a stranger to me. I cannot give money to strangers."

"But I tell you it was paid to you without authority."

"Did he not have his mother's authority?"

"His mother has nothing to say. I am the boss in my own house."

"Possibly, but the rooms which I let to Mrs. Manton belong to her, not to you."

"I see how it is," said Gerrish roughly, "you want to keep the money."

"My dear sir, I intend to keep the money," said the agent significantly.

"But it is not due you yet."

"Then send Mrs. Manton round to ask it back. I shouldn't feel bound to give it back, mind you, but if she wanted it particularly I might do so."

"Look here, Mr. Agent," said Gerrish insolently, "that don't go down."

"I fail to understand your meaning," answered the agent in a quieter tone, but his mouth was compressed, and he was clearly getting out of patience with his visitor.

"Then I'll make myself understood. Give me back that five dollars or I'll make you."

"Indeed!"

"Yes, indeed!" said Gerrish in a tone of mockery.

He surveyed the agent with contempt. Mr. Duncan was not so tall as he, and probably weighed twenty pounds less. He did not know however that the agent belonged to an athletic club, and excelled in the games peculiar to Scotland.

"Why," thought Gerrish, "I can chaw him up if I like."

"I have only a word or two to say to you, Mr. Gerrish," said Duncan, stepping from behind the office table. "Leave this office as soon as possible."

"I'll leave when I get ready," was the impudent reply.

"Then I shall put you out!"

"Ho, ho!" laughed Gerrish. "What a good one! I'd like to see you do it."

"I shall be happy to accommodate you."

He seized Gerrish by the shoulders, and before that gentleman had a very clear idea of what was going on, he found himself thrown out on the sidewalk and the door closed behind him.

"Good morning, Mr. Gerrish," said Duncan ceremoniously. "You had better not call again. I prefer to transact business with Mrs. Manton or Frank."

"What have I struck?" soliloquized Gerrish in a dazed tone. "The little man has muscles of iron. I didn't think he was so strong. Blest if I'd have tackled him if I'd have known he was a steam engine in breeches."

Here was a second defeat for Gerrish. He began to think that there was no luck for him. All his plans of living without labor had miscarried, and he began to feel the inconvenience of being penniless. For some years he had been saved any anxiety about meeting the expense of board and lodging, as the State of New York had generously provided for him and sent him no bill. Now that he was a free man, he found his appetite inconvenient. His wife and stepson did not feel disposed to contribute to his support. Luke felt that this was hard.

He unbosomed himself to Jack Dumont, with whom he lodged.

"When I married that woman," he said, bitterly, "I thought she had a heart. I didn't think she'd turn from me so coldly after my sufferings in that den up the river."

"Possibly," said Dumont with mild sarcasm, "she thought it was your place to support her."

"Very likely, very likely! Some women are very selfish. Don't you ever marry, Jack. You'll repent it."

"I shall find out first if the woman is able to support a husband. So Mrs. G. and her son have proved too much for you."

"Not yet!" returned Gerrish, striking the table beside him with his clenched fist. "They won't get off so easily."

"What shall you do next?"

"The boy will receive his pay Saturday afternoon. I hear the office closes at five. I shall be on hand and relieve him of it."

"He doesn't look like a boy that would submit quietly."

"He'll have to submit!" growled Gerrish.

"He is a stout, strong boy."

"I am bigger and stronger," remarked Gerrish, complacently. "I'll tell you what, Jack, I'll invite you to take dinner with me Saturday evening. You can choose the place yourself, and we'll have a good time."

"Say, Delmonico's," suggested Dumont, jocosely.

"Not this time."

"I know a place where for seventy five cents we can get a nice dinner of six courses with wine."

"That will do. Consider yourself engaged."

"I will. I don't think I have any other engagement that evening. Let me see, it is on Friday I am to dine with the mayor, so that won't interfere."

Both laughed at this not very brilliant joke. On the strength of the anticipated dinner Dumont lent Gerrish fifty cents, which that gentleman promised to pay back promptly.

The same evening Frank met Mr. Duncan, the real estate agent, and obtained from him an account of his stepfather's call and what came of it.

"So he actually wanted you to pay back the five dollars!" exclaimed Frank. "Why can't he work, a great, strong man like him?"

"He didn't feel very strong when he was in my grasp," chuckled Duncan.

Frank eyed the agent with curiosity.

"I shouldn't have thought you could have handled him," he said. "He is larger and heavier than you."

"That's true, lad, but he hasn't the science," replied the Scotchman.

"I hope you won't use any of your science on me, Mr. Duncan."

"No fear, lad," said the agent, laying his hand kindly on the boy's shoulder. "You're a good lad, and a good son, and if ever Aleck Duncan can do you a good turn, he will. We Scotchmen are a little close, mayhap, but we look out for our own, and we feel kindly to those who are good to their mothers."

"Thank you, Mr. Duncan, for your friendliness. I hope I shan't need help, but I may need advice, and if I do there is no one I will come to so readily as you."

"Shake hands on it, lad."

Frank extended his hand, and the agent pressed it warmly.

"Do right, lad," he said, "and the Lord will take care of you."

"I wish he would put it into the heart of Mr. Gerrish to go away and leave us alone."

"Don't be impatient! That'll come in good time. Luke Gerrish is sure to get into trouble. He doesn't want to work, and such men are likely to fall into temptation."

Frank was cheered by the kindness and approval of Alexander Duncan. He was not a man of magnetic manners, nor likely to win general attachment, but he possessed sterling qualities, and his heart was softer than was commonly supposed.

On Saturday afternoon, at the close of business hours, Frank received his week's salary, now advanced to five dollars. It so happened that he received it on this occasion from Gideon Chapin.

"Mind you don't spend it foolishly!" said Chapin, harshly.

"Your advice is good, Mr. Chapin," said Frank quietly. "If you speak as a friend I thank you for it."

The face of the old clerk did not look over friendly, and he made no answer.

Frank left the store. At the next corner Luke Gerrish met him and seized him roughly by the arm.

"You've been paid off," he said. "Give me the money!"

CHAPTER XI.

A FRIEND IN NEED.

Frank was taken by surprise, but instinctively tried to throw off the grasp of his stepfather.

"Let me alone!" he said.

"You heard what I said? Give me your wages."

By this time Frank had recovered his self possession, and faced Luke Gerrish resolutely.

"I will not do it," he said. "You have not the least claim to my wages."

"You will find out whether I have or not. Ain't I your stepfather?"

"I suppose so."

"You only suppose so! Don't you know it?"

"Yes," burst forth Frank, "I know it, and am ashamed of it."

"Ashamed of me, are you? I'll pay you for that. Give me that money."

Frank's reply was to button up his coat.

"You will have to get money somewhere else, Mr. Gerrish," he said. "I tell you once for all that you won't get it from me."

Luke was by this time out of patience. He was not at the best a good tempered man, and it was very aggravating to be defied by a boy of sixteen, upon whom he fancied he had a claim for obedience.

In a savage fit he aimed a blow at Frank which would have hurt the boy seriously if it had fallen. But his arm was seized in a strong grasp. Turning quickly to see who had interfered with him, he met the steady look of a man of thirty eight, or perhaps a little older. This man was evidently a gentleman—in the social sense of that term—for he was handsomely dressed, and had that quiet air of authority which comes from acknowledged position.

"What do you mean by interfering with me?" demanded Gerrish, almost foaming at the mouth with passion.

"I mean to protect this boy from your brutality. Did I hear you demanding money from him?"

"Yes, you did."

"I have a great mind to hand you over to a policeman."

"What for?"

"Attempted robbery."

"Then you'd make a fool of yourself. I have a right to the boy's wages."

"Why?"

"Because I am his father."

"Is this true?" asked the gentleman, looking with surprise from the coarse, sensual face of Luke Gerrish to the handsome and refined features of Frank Manton.

Frank blushed with shame.

"He is my stepfather," answered Frank, "but till a few days since I had not seen him for five years."

"He was out of the country?"

"No, sir; he was at Sing Sing prison."

"I'll get even with you for saying that!" interrupted Gerrish angrily.

"Since he came out," continued Frank, "he has tried to extort money from mother and myself. He went to Mr. Snobden, my employer, and asked that my weekly wages should be paid to him. Mr. Snobden refused, and now he has tried to collect them himself."

"I see. Do you carry them to your mother?"

"Yes, sir."

"That is right. It is what I did when I was a boy."

"My mother is poor, and needs all the help I can give."

"So was mine. You look surprised. Why?"

"Because you seem like a rich man."

"I am rich, but I was a poor boy. I lived in the country, in a town about thirty miles distant on the Erie road. My father was a farmer, and I a farmer's son."

"You don't look a farmer now, sir."

"No; I am a banker."

"Then, sir, if you are rich," whined Gerrish, "I hope you will have pity on a poor man who is out of luck."

"Do you mean yourself?"

"Yes, sir; I haven't a penny in my pocket, and I have had nothing to eat all day."

The gentleman turned away with an expression of disgust.

"I don't believe a word you say," he said sharply.

"Won't you tell the boy to give me a quarter?"

"No; you don't deserve it. You are strong and able bodied. There is no reason why you should not earn your own living."

"I can't get work," whined Gerrish.

"Have you tried?"

"Yes, sir."

"Then I will give you a job. I live at No. 75 West Forty Eighth Street. Two tons of coal will be delivered at my house in an hour. Go up there, and I will give you the job of putting it in the cellar, and pay you seventy five cents. What do you say?"

"Would you mind paying a part of the money in advance?" added Gerrish.

"Yes, I should mind it. I don't like the principle of paying in advance unless there is a special need."

"There is in my case, sir. I have had nothing to eat today, and I am afraid I should not have strength enough for the job. If you will let me have a quarter, I will go into a restaurant and get a little supper, and then go right up to your house."

"That will be unnecessary. I will leave orders in the kitchen that you are to be supplied with supper."

"Thank you, sir," said Gerrish, as he walked away. "You may expect me;" but he did not look particularly well pleased.

"He won't come," said the gentleman, turning to Frank with a smile.

"No, sir, I don't think he will. He would rather live without work."

"I have met with plenty of his stripe. I am sorry you are connected with such a man. Does he annoy you much?"

"Yes, sir. I am always afraid he will call and trouble my mother while I am away."

"For whom do you work?"

"For Silas Snobden."

"I remember. Do you like the place?"

"Pretty well, sir."

"How do you like Mr. Snobden? I ask because I know him in business."

"He is not a very agreeable man. He is very strict, and sometimes finds fault, but on the whole he is just, and not unreasonable."

"That is well. How much does he pay you?"

"Till this week, four dollars. I am now to receive five."

"And this money you give to your mother? Has she any property?"

"No, sir."

"Surely you two can't live on five dollars a week."

"Mother earns a little—about a dollar and a half a week."

"That makes six dollars and a half. You must have to manage very closely."

"So we do, but we won't complain if Mr. Gerrish will keep away. We can't support him too."

"Of course not."

"I have been thinking that I could put in your coal if you would pay me what you offered my stepfather," said Frank.

"First, let me ask you a question. What sort of an education have you?"

"Pretty fair, sir. I managed to attend school till I was fourteen, and then I was ready to enter the New York College. I passed the examination, but found when the term began that I could not spare the time required."

"Are you fond of children?"

"Yes, sir; I can always get along with them."

"You don't consider them a nuisance?"

"No, sir."

Frank was surprised by these questions. He could not think what his companion was driving at. The explanation was soon given.

"I have a boy about eight years of age," said the banker, "who has been delicate from birth. We have been obliged to be unusually careful of him. He has not been able to associate much with boys of his own age, or to engage in the usual sports of boyhood. He is my only child," he continued, with a sigh, "and to make the poor boy's lot worse, his mother is dead. When I am at home in the evening, he is in my company, but I am often called away. Now it has occurred to me that he would enjoy the company of one who, though older, is still a boy. How would you like to come up every evening and stay with him from seven to nine o'clock?"

"Very much, sir, if you think he would like it."

"I feel sure he would."

"When do you wish me to begin?"

"Can you come up this evening?"

"Yes, sir."

"I will give you five dollars a week—the same sum you receive from Mr. Snobden. Will that be satisfactory?"

Frank's eyes sparkled.

"Why, I shall be earning ten dollars a week."

"You will be able to make your mother more comfortable."

"Indeed I shall."

"Then I shall expect you at seven. Here is my card."

Frank took the card, and found this name engraved upon it.

MR. ALLEN PALMER.

The name was familiar to him, and he remembered now once going to Mr. Palmer's office in Wall Street with a letter from Mr. Snobden.

CHAPTER XII.

AN OLD FASHIONED BOY.

The banker proceeded to the nearest station of the Sixth Avenue Elevated Road, and boarded a train which in a few minutes landed him at Fiftieth Street. It was a short walk to his own house.

Somewhere near the center of the block, between Fifth and Sixth Avenues, is a handsome brown stone dwelling four stories in height. The banker ascended the steps, and taking a pass key from his pocket, admitted himself.

His approach had not been unobserved. A small boy had been watching from one of the front windows with his face glued to the pane for at least half an hour.

"Good evening, papa!" he exclaimed joyfully, "I have been watching for you a long time."

"I am later than usual, Rob," said Mr. Palmer, stooping down and kissing the boy fondly. "I was detained, but here I am at last!"

"I am so glad to see you, papa!"

"And I am glad to see you, my dear little boy. Tell me, have you been lonely today?"

"I am always lonely when you are away, papa. Shall you be at home this evening?"

"I am sorry to say, Rob, that I must go away a little before eight. I am invited to meet a prominent Englishman at the house of a friend."

Rob sighed, but he made no complaint.

"Then I will go to bed at eight," he said.

"No, I don't think you will," said his father with a smile.

"Why not, papa?" asked the little boy, in surprise.

"Because you are going to have company. It would not be polite to go to bed, and leave your company, would it?"

"Surely not, papa. But who is it?"

"It is a boy—of sixteen."

"What is his name?"

"Frank Manton."

"Do you think I will like him? Why is he coming to see me?"

"Because I think he will be company for you. He will come every evening and stay from seven to nine if you like him. He will read to you, play games with you, and in fact he will be at your service."

"But will he be willing to give me so much of his time?"

"Listen, Rob; he is a poor boy, and has a mother to support. I shall pay him five dollars a week, and that will help him a great deal. Shall I tell you how and where I met him?"

"Do, papa."

"He had just been paid his week's wages by a merchant in White Street, who employs him, when his stepfather, a coarse looking man, met him on the sidewalk and tried to force his wages from him."

"And did he succeed?" asked Rob, who was becoming very much interested.

"He might have done so, if I had not come to his assistance. I seized him by the arm, and made him let the boy go."

"Good, papa!"

"The stepfather, Frank told me, is only just out of Sing Sing prison. He looks like a criminal. No sooner was he released than he found out his wife and stepson, and tried to extort money from them, so that he could live without work."

"What a wicked man!"

"No man without self respect would be willing to live on the scanty earnings of a woman and a boy, even if he were related to them."

"Unless he was sick and feeble."

"True! But this man is strong and robust, but unwilling to work. After I interfered with him he begged me to give him some money, judging from my appearance that I was rich."

"Did you give him any?"

"No, but I told him that if he would come up to the house I would employ him to put in some coal which I had ordered. I offered him seventy five cents."

"Then I shall see him."

"No, for I am sure he won't come. Such men as he won't work unless they are actually obliged to."

"Is Frank a nice boy?" asked Rob with interest.

"He is a very good looking boy, and he looks good, which is still better."

"He must be a good boy if he helps his mother."

"Tell me, Rob, if I were to grow poor would you be willing to work for me?"

"Wouldn't I, papa? But I am afraid I couldn't do much. You know I am not very strong."

As Allen Palmer's eye fell thoughtfully on the little boy's fragile figure, and thin face, he had to keep back tears of sadness—but he controlled himself and said as cheerfully as he could—"You are young yet, Rob, and there is plenty of time to grow stout and strong."

"Papa," said the little boy thoughtfully, "you won't mind it much if I tell you a secret." .

"No, my dear boy!"

"I am almost certain that I shall never live to be a man!"

"What makes you say that, Rob?" said his father quickly. "Have you been feeling ill lately?"

"No, papa, not more so than usual."

"Then what could have put such a thought into your head?"

"I don't know, but when Cousin Eugene was here last week he began to tell me what he meant to do when he was a man. Now I never look forward to that. I never expect to live long enough for that."

"But, Rob," said Mr. Palmer, "you mustn't give way to such thoughts as that. Think of the bright side. I don't want you to sadden yourself with thoughts of death."

"They don't make me sad, papa. Of course I should not like to leave you, but I should be with dear mamma in Heaven, you know."

Man as he was Allen Palmer had hard work to suppress a sob, as he listened to these touching words of the child whom he loved all the better on account of his weakness.

"You are an old fashioned boy," he said at length. "I see what has been putting these morbid fancies into your little mind."

"What, papa?"

"Your being so much alone. I am all the more glad that I have engaged you a young and lively companion. Frank Manton is strong and full of life. You won't think of an early death when he is with you."

"I think I shall like him, papa, from what you tell me."

"I hope you will, Rob."

They had not risen from the dinner table when the bell rang, and Katy entering said, "There's a boy wants to see you, Mr. Palmer. He says you told him to call."

"It is all right. Bring him in."

"In here, sir?"

"Yes."

A minute later Frank entered the dining room.

"Good evening, sir!" he said with modest self possession.

"Good evening, Frank. This is my little boy, Robert, commonly called Rob."

"Good evening, Rob," said Frank advancing with a smile, and taking the little boy's hand.

Rob was instantly attracted by his bright face and pleasant manner.

"Good evening!" he said. "Won't you sit down and have some ice cream?"

"Well thought of, Rob. Katy, set a plate for Master Frank, and serve him with ice cream."

Frank seated himself beside Rob, and ate the cream with relish—what boy isn't fond of ice cream?

"How old are you, Frank?" asked Rob.

"Sixteen."

"You are just twice as old as I am. I don't think I shall ever be as large and strong as you."

"Oh yes you will, Rob," said Frank cheerfully. "Why I know a man that weighs two hundred pounds, and from what he tells me he wasn't any bigger than you when he was eight."

"There, Rob, you see the prospect before you," said his father. "Some time you may be a big man weighing two hundred pounds."

The little fellow burst into a hearty laugh that gladdened his father's heart.

"The boy is already doing him good," he thought. "It was a lucky idea of mine to engage him."

When they rose from the table Rob offered to show Frank his books and curiosities. The young boy had a spacious chamber on the third floor which seemed ludicrously out of proportion to his small figure. His father's love had supplied him with a library of a hundred and fifty juvenile and historical books, and numberless pictures and ornaments.

"What a beautiful room you have!" said Frank admiringly. "What a good father you must have!"

"Isn't he though? He tells me," Rob added hesitatingly, "that you have a bad stepfather. Do you mind telling me about him?"

"Not at all. Sit down and I'll tell you all about him."

Rob was intensely interested in this life story of his new

friend. He plied Frank with questions, and that evening made the two boys firm friends.

When nine o'clock came and Frank prepared to go, Rob said, "You'll be sure to come tomorrow evening?"

"Yes, Rob, I shall be glad to do so."

"I like you very much, Frank. Papa said I would," and he placed his little hand confidingly in Frank's.

The next morning at the breakfast table Mr. Palmer said, "Rob, do you like Frank?"

"I *love* him, papa. What a wicked man Luke Gerrish is!"

"And who is Luke Gerrish?"

"His stepfather."

"I made no mistake," thought the banker. "That boy will do him good."

CHAPTER XIII.

GIDEON CHAPIN AND HIS NEPHEW.

Among the thousands who live in Brooklyn while doing business in New York was Gideon Chapin, already introduced as head of a department in the establishment of Silas Snobden.

At half past five o'clock in the afternoon he entered a ferry boat at the foot of Fulton Street. He passed through into the second cabin and sat down. A boy of sixteen crossed from the opposite side and took a seat next him.

"Hello, Uncle Gideon," he said.

"Oh it's you, is it, Benson?"

"Yes, uncle."

"Where have you been?"

"I went over to New York to see if I could get a position."

"What luck did you have?"

"None at all. In one place they asked for my reference. When I mentioned you, and said that you were head of a department at Snobden's the merchant said, 'Why doesn't your uncle get you into his store?' "

"Well, what did you say?"

"That there was no vacancy at present."

"Well?"

"Then he said, 'There must be some objection against you, or he would manage it somehow.' "

"That doesn't follow."

"Really, Uncle Gideon, I think you could manage it if you tried hard."

"Perhaps you know better than I," answered Gideon, peevishly.

"Haven't you been there a long time?"

"Yes."

"Then, if you should tell them you wouldn't stay unless they took me I'd get in."

"So that's your idea, is it? Suppose they should take me at my word?"

"They wouldn't let you go, would they?"

"Mr. Snobden would let any one go that put on airs. You don't know what sort of man he is."

"You have always got along well with him."

"Yes, because I minded my own business."

Benson Tyler looked disappointed.

"Then is there no hope for me?" he asked.

"Yes, if you will give me time. I have already mentioned you to Mr. Snobden, and he has promised to take you whenever there is a vacancy."

"Is there likely to be?"

"I can't say. At present we have a boy."

"What is his name?"

"Frank Manton."

"What sort of a boy is he?"

"I don't like him. He doesn't treat me with proper respect."

"How long has he been there?"

"About a year."

"How much is he paid?"

"He has just been raised to five dollars."

"Then old Snobden likes him," said Benson, looking sober.

"Yes, as long as he behaves well. But as soon as he commits a serious fault, he will have to go. Snobden has no mercy in such cases."

"Couldn't you manage to get him bounced?"

"I thought I had a hold on him the other day when I saw him

walking down Broadway with a disreputable looking fellow. I called the attention of Mr. Snobden to this, but the boy was able to prove that the man was a nephew to Snobden himself, who was trying to pump him about his employer. Of course that cleared him, and put me in an embarrassing position."

"Hasn't the boy got any bad habits?" asked Benson.

"If he has he is artful enough to keep them hidden. Mr. Snobden said the other day that he was the best office boy he had ever had."

By this time they had reached the Brooklyn side, and walked to a small house on Cranberry Street where Benson lived with his widowed mother. Mr. Chapin occupied a room in his sister's house, and the sum he paid for board and lodging was more than sufficient to pay the rent of the whole house.

"Uncle Gideon," said Benson, as they ascended the front steps, "can you lend me a quarter?"

"What for?" asked Gideon, frowning.

He was a close man, and never lent or gave away money willingly.

"I want to go to the theater tonight."

"Very well! You can stay at home. When you earn a salary, you can go on your own money."

"I should like to do it, but I can't get a place."

"Go and sell afternoon papers, then. I did at your age."

The door was opened, and this advice was heard by Benson's mother, a tall, thin woman, with corkscrew curls, who was in a chronic state of discontent, and showed it in her face.

"Gideon!" she said impatiently, "what was that you said?"

"I was advising Benson to sell papers if he had no other way of earning money."

"Would you have my son, and your nephew, a common newsboy?" exclaimed the lady, indignantly.

"There are boys just as good as he that sell papers."

"He won't do it with my consent."

"I guess I'll have to if I want any money to spend like other boys," grumbled Benson. "I only want a quarter."

"I'll try to raise it for you," said Mrs. Tyler, with a sharp glance at her brother. "If I had a large income like your uncle I would see that you had a little recreation now and then."

"I suppose that is a hint for me, Petronella," said Gideon Chapin grimly.

"I shall not give any hints," said Mrs. Tyler. "I do not care to have you oblige Benson if you are unwilling. I am a poor widow, or the poor boy would fare better."

"One would think I was a mean skinflint by the way you two talk," said Gideon, irritably.

"If Benson were only earning something, I would not annoy you so much," said Mrs. Tyler, pathetically putting her handkerchief to her eyes.

"Why doesn't the boy look for a place in Brooklyn?"

"He can't find any, poor boy! He meets with rebuffs on all hands. It is his earnest wish to be with you, but you don't try to help him."

"You do me injustice, Petronella. I tried only this week, but without success."

"Where there's a will there's a way."

"Is there? Not always. If I should take a fancy to buy a brown stone house on Madison Avenue, New York, I suppose you would say that."

"I will say nothing more, Gideon. Only remember that Benson is fatherless. If his poor father were living he would have some one to push him upward."

"Say no more, Petronella. I see that there will be no peace for me till I have secured that position for Benson. I will do it by hook or by crook if it is a possible thing to do."

"There speaks my good brother!" said the lady, deigning to be appeased.

"Can you spare a quarter for me, uncle?" asked Benson, thinking it a good time to strike another blow.

"Yes, yes, there it is!" and Mr. Chapin tossed him the silver coin he desired.

When Gideon came down to supper his sister smiled upon him graciously.

"I have made some cream toast for you, Gideon," she said. "I knew you liked it. If there is any particular dish you want at any time let me know, and I will get it if it is a possible thing."

"You are very kind, Petronella."

"Why should I not be, Gideon? You are my only brother. You and Benson are the only two beings for whom I care to live. I could not bear to part with you."

"You won't have to, Petronella, unless I should take a fancy to get married."

"Do you think of it?" asked his sister aghast.

"Well, not at present."

"I hope not. When a man gets to be fifty one marriage is very hazardous."

"It always is!" growled Gideon, sipping his tea. "I'm sure I've often heard Benson's father say——"

"What?" demanded his sister, her eyes flashing ominously.

"That he never would have married, if—he hadn't met you!"

"Yes," sighed Petronella. "George and I were very happy together."

Gideon Chapin shrugged his shoulders. It would not do, as he very well knew, to contradict his sister on such a point.

That night he set his wits to work to devise a scheme for getting rid of Frank at the office. At length one occurred to him which seemed feasible.

CHAPTER XIV.

BENSON VISITS HIS UNCLE.

Frank did not mention at the store his evening engagement. He thought it might possibly be made an excuse for reducing his salary. Mr. Snobden was a man who did not like to have his employees earn too much. One of his clerks in an unguarded moment told him that he had inherited eight hundred dollars from an uncle. The next Saturday he found his salary docked two dollars a week.

"Why have you reduced my salary, Mr. Snobden?" he asked indignantly. "Do I not give you satisfaction?"

"Oh, you do fairly well," said Silas Snobden cautiously, for he did not think it politic to praise his clerks.

"Don't you think I am as deserving as last week?"

"The fact is, Mr. Warren, clerks generally receive too high wages—you among them—but I hesitated in reducing your pay, because I thought you might find it hard to get along. Now, however, that you have received such a handsome legacy I no longer hesitate. You can afford to take less."

"But, Mr. Snobden, is this fair? What has my legacy to do with the salary you pay me?"

"Mr. Warren, I have not time to discuss the matter. Of course, if you have a chance to better yourself elsewhere, I won't interfere or hold you back."

Warren left the office, regretting bitterly that he had not kept to himself the secret of his good fortune.

"I didn't think Silas Snobden was quite so mean," he said

to his wife in the evening. "To make Uncle Tom's money pay part of my wages, and he rolling in wealth."

"I wouldn't stay in his employ," said his wife indignantly.

"New situations are not to be picked up every day, Margaret. I shall stay where I am till I get a better offer, and then I will tender my resignation to old Snobden. It will be a joyful day when I can do it."

So Frank kept about his daily work in the same way as he had hitherto done. He could not help noticing that Gideon Chapin seemed to be watching him closely, and, it was clear, with no friendly eyes. It annoyed him, and he determined to let Mr. Chapin know it.

So one day when the old clerk was at leisure, Frank walked up to him boldly and asked, "Why is it, Mr. Chapin, that you are watching me continually?"

Chapin was rather taken aback by the boy's boldness.

"Who told you I was watching you?" he asked.

"I can't help seeing it."

"Then you must be watching me."

"No, sir; but I keep my eyes open."

"Then you object to being watched?" said Gideon, with a sneer.

"It isn't comfortable to be under watch all the time."

"Boys need watching," said Chapin, sententiously. "Only those who have something to conceal object to it."

"I have nothing to conceal," rejoined Frank warmly.

"I am very glad to hear it," answered Chapin dryly. "I am not surprised to hear you say so. I presume most boys would do the same."

"Do men ever need watching?" asked Frank.

"Sometimes. A boy who needs watching also needs watching when he is a man."

"Has Mr. Snobden asked you to watch me?"

"You must excuse my saying anything on that point. If you are all right it won't do you any harm to be watched."

And this was all the satisfaction that Frank could get. He did not complain to Mr. Snobden, for that gentleman was well understood to be cranky, and there was no knowing how he would take it.

Frank did not understand why it was that Mr. Chapin displayed such hostility to him, but he was soon to be enlightened.

One morning as he was entering White Street from Broadway he was accosted by a boy about his own age, who asked, "Can you tell me where Mr. Snobden's place of business is?"

"Yes," answered Frank, "that is where I am going."

"Are you in his employ?" asked the boy, eying Frank curiously.

"Yes."

"I have an uncle who has been a clerk there for many years."

"Who is it? I know all who are there."

"Mr. Gideon Chapin."

"Oh!" said Frank, beginning to understand.

"He lives at my mother's house in Brooklyn."

"I believe he is one of the oldest clerks—I mean he has been there as long as any one."

"So Uncle Gideon says. I expect to work for Mr. Snobden myself some time. Uncle Gideon says he will try to get me in."

"Just as I supposed," thought Frank, and he scanned his new acquaintance critically.

"May I ask your name?" he said.

"Benson Tyler. You, I suppose, are Frank Manton."

"Yes," answered Frank, surprised. "I did not suppose you would know my name."

"I have heard Uncle Gideon speak of you."

"I'll be bound he didn't say anything good of me," thought Frank.

"How much wages do you get?"

"Five dollars a week," answered Frank.

"That is pretty good."

"Yes, I don't complain of it. But here we are at the store. Shall I conduct you to your uncle?"

"If you like. Uncle told me he would take me to lunch."

Gideon Chapin was at work in the back part of the store. Frank led Benson to him, and pointing him out left him.

"Well, Uncle Gideon, here I am!" said Benson.

"I see. Where did you pick up Frank Manton?"

"Outside, just as I was turning in from Broadway."

"Humph! what do you think of him?"

"I don't fancy him much. He seems stuck up."

"You are right, though he has nothing to boast of. His mother is poor, and he has for a stepfather a disreputable looking old tramp who came here one day and tried to get his wages."

"Did he succeed?"

"No, Mr. Snobden had him put out of the store."

"I shouldn't think Mr. Snobden would want the son of such a man in his employ?"

"I agree with you. If I had my way I would discharge the boy tomorrow. Benson, that is the boy who stands between you and a situation here."

Benson frowned and looked angry.

"I should think you would have influence enough with the old man to get him out."

"Hush!" said Gideon Chapin cautiously. "Don't speak of Mr. Snobden in that way in the store. If you were overheard, and it should be reported to him, that would end all your chances of being employed here. By the way, I must take you into the office and introduce you to Mr. Snobden. It will be well for him to have seen you in case—there is a vacancy."

"All right, Uncle Gideon."

"You must speak very politely, and be very respectful. First impressions go a long way, Benson."

"Oh, I know how to behave," said Benson flippantly. "Don't you be afraid for me."

"I am glad you do know how to behave," said Gideon, sharply. "There are times at home when I have been led to doubt it."

"Oh, a fellow can't always be on his good behavior."

"Well, you'd better be now at any rate. You can come with me as Mr. Snobden appears to be at leisure."

He walked to the other end of the room and entered the inner office, with Benson closely following him.

"Well, Mr. Chapin?" said the merchant, looking up from his desk.

"I beg your pardon for the liberty, Mr. Snobden," said Gideon Chapin, in a cringing manner, "but I wanted to introduce to you my nephew, Benson Tyler, of Brooklyn."

"Ha! Is that the boy?"

"Yes, Benson!"

This last was in a tone of admonition. Benson took the hint, and bowing, said, "Good morning, Mr. Snobden!"

"Good morning, boy. How old are you?"

"Sixteen, sir."

"Just the age of Frank Manton," suggested Gideon.

"Ha! I see. Are you attending school?"

"I have been, sir; but now I am looking for a place."

"Are there no places to be had in Brooklyn?"

"Yes, Mr. Snobden," said Gideon, "but I prefer that Benson should take a place in New York. There is more chance to rise. If, now, Frank Manton should leave you, I should make bold to mention Benson as his successor."

"But Frank Manton has no intention of leaving, has he?"

"Not that I am aware of," answered Gideon, coughing.

"Then there is nothing to be said."

"You'll excuse my bringing in my nephew, Mr. Snobden. He has heard so much of you, as one of the leading merchants of New York, that he wished to see you."

"Very well!" said Mr. Snobden, more graciously, for he was not insensible to flattery. "I am glad to see the young man."

"Come, Benson, we mustn't waste any more of Mr. Snobden's valuable time. You can come out to lunch with me."

As they left the store Benson said, "What a disagreeable looking man Mr. Snobden is! He looks like a crank."

"Be careful what you say, Benson. I mean you to be his office boy, and that very soon."

CHAPTER XV.

THE PLOT AGAINST FRANK.

Several days passed. Gideon Chapin thought it politic to wait awhile before carrying out his scheme against Frank. Just after his introduction of Benson to Mr. Snobden, it might have looked suspicious.

But one morning at breakfast he said significantly to his nephew: "Benson, I advise you to come round to the store at eleven o'clock this forenoon."

"I have another engagement, Uncle Gideon," said Benson uneasily.

"You have?" said his uncle sharply. "I suppose it is a very important one."

"Well, me and another fellow are going to Prospect Park."

"Very important, upon my word! By the way, were you taught at school to say *me* and another fellow?"

"Well, I and another fellow. Of course I know better, but a fellow can't always be thinking of his grammar."

"It would be more becoming to say another fellow and I."

"Is it very important for Benson to call on you today?" asked Mrs. Tyler, who was weakly indulgent to her son.

"As to that, I had hopes of getting him into Mr. Snobden's employment today, but if you don't think it of any importance, let him go to Prospect Park, by all means."

"Oh, Gideon, of course that alters matters. Benson, my darling, of course you will do as your uncle wishes."

"I don't mind, mother," said Benson, who was really desirous of the place, "but don't call me darling! It makes me feel as young as little Lord Fauntleroy."

"Oh, my son, how little you appreciate a mother's fondness!"

"That's all right, but I wouldn't have any of the fellows hear you call me darling for the world."

"Benson is right," said Gideon Chapin. "He is too old to be addressed in that way. You never hear *me* call him darling!"

Benson burst into an hysterical giggle. The very idea of his prim, dignified uncle calling him darling seemed to him irresistibly funny.

Even Gideon smiled at the thought.

"Well," he said, as he took his hat to go, "I shall expect you, Benson. If you don't come, never expect me to make another effort to get you into the store."

"But how are you going to do it, uncle?" asked Benson curiously. "Is Frank Manton going to be discharged?"

"I expect so."

"What has he done?"

"Don't be too curious! Leave me to manage that."

"When did you find out that he had been doing something out of the way?"

"I don't care to answer any questions. Come over at eleven o'clock. That will be all you have to do."

"I should like to see how Frank Manton looks when he is discharged," chuckled Benson.

"You don't like him, then?"

"No. He's a chump."

"That settles it. I don't know what a chump is, but no doubt it is something bad," remarked Gideon dryly.

He reached his place of business a little earlier than usual. A young fellow about twenty years of age came up to him and handed him a sheet of note paper, folded as if it came out of an envelope. Mr. Chapin cast his eyes over it.

"That will do, Higgins," he said. "I think you asked me to lend you five dollars."

"Yes, sir."

"Here it is. Now mind you keep your mouth shut, and I won't report your carelessness of last week."

"All right, sir! Thank you."

"I wonder what he is going to do with that letter," thought the young man. "I suppose he is going to get Frank Manton into trouble. I am sorry I wrote the letter for him. It's mean, I know, but he might have got me discharged. Besides, the five dollars will come in handy."

About quarter of eleven Gideon Chapin made his way to the office, where Mr. Snobden was seated as usual at his desk. Frank Manton had just gone out on an errand, so the occasion seemed propitious.

"Ahem!" coughed Gideon, as he entered the office gingerly.

"Well, Chapin, what's wanted?"

"I have come on an unpleasant errand, Mr. Snobden."

"What is it—to ask to have your salary raised? That would be unpleasant, and it would be of no use."

"No, Mr. Snobden, no sir, I don't complain of my salary. You are always just—and generous."

"Am I?" returned Snobden dryly. "I am glad to hear you say so. I have the impression that some persons in my employ express themselves differently. It is rather a relief to find that one man is of a different opinion."

"I am always faithful and loyal, Mr. Snobden, always faithful and loyal," said Gideon, rubbing his hands after the fashion of an English tradesman. Mr. Chapin, by the way, was born in London, and had been brought to America in his boyhood.

"Glad to hear it, but that isn't what you came to tell me!"

"No, sir. I will come to the point. I know that your time is valuable. I have a document here that was found on the floor of the warehouse which reflects heavily on your office boy, Frank Manton."

"What! Frank Manton in trouble! Give me the document, as you call it."

Mr. Chapin took from his pocket the paper which had been handed him by young Higgins, and placed it in the hands of Mr. Snobden. We will look over his shoulder as he reads it:

FRANK: I wish you would pay me that five dollars I won from you at poker the other night. I'm terribly hard up, and need it right off. I got hit hard last evening in a game with Gene Buckner, and if I don't pay up he'll give me away to my boss, and that'll just ruin me. If you haven't got the money, you'll run a chance of finding some loose money round in the office. Old Snobden is so rich that he won't miss it. Any way, let me see you this evening at the corner of Thirteenth Street and Third Avenue, and be sure to bring me something.

Your old pal,
JIMMY KEEFE.

P. S.—I saw your stepfather last evening coming out of a drinking saloon. He's a nice man to have in a family.

"What does this mean, Mr. Chapin?" added Silas Snobden, looking up from the note.

"Why, sir, it appears to be a confidential letter to your office boy from some dissolute companion of his. It seems that Frank Manton is in the habit of playing poker, and owes the fellow five dollars. That is what I make out of it."

Silas Snobden cast his eyes over it again.

"It looks like that," he said. "Where did you find the letter?"

"I didn't find it."

"Who, then?"

"It was found by a young man employed in the back of the store—John Higgins."

"When did he find it?"

"Last evening, I believe. He was kept at work a little later than usual. He brought it to me this morning."

"Do you think my office boy dropped it? Why couldn't it have been some other Frank?"

"Just what occurred to me, sir. I didn't like to think badly of young Manton, and gave him the benefit of that doubt. But the postscript seems to make it clear that he was meant, and no other."

"About the stepfather?"

"Yes, sir."

"Humph! I wouldn't have supposed Frank was a poker player. He seems a very steady, moral boy."

"So he does, Mr. Snobden, so he does. And perhaps he can explain it. I fervently hope that he can, though I cannot conceive in what manner. Of course I need not say that a poker player cannot be trusted. Sooner or later he will be tempted to dishonesty. I am glad to say that my nephew, Benson Tyler —I introduced him to you last week—has no faults of that description. His mother and I—the poor fellow has lost his father —have reared him strictly, and watched him closely in his budding boyhood, till I can confidently speak of him as a model young man. He is just the age of Frank Manton."

"Humph! he is not in a place?" inquired Snobden, catching at the bait.

"No, sir; he has an offer from a Brooklyn man, but I would rather have him in New York. Bless my soul! there he comes!" said Gideon, looking to the door through which Benson was just entering. "I will go and speak to him."

"Keep him here for a while, Mr. Chapin. I may wish to speak to him."

"Yes, sir."

"And—keep this discovery to yourself. When Frank Manton comes back from his errand I will speak to him."

"Yes, sir."

"I think I have fired the train that will land Frank Manton in the street," said Gideon, smiling softly to himself. "Nothing like strategy, Gideon Chapin—nothing like strategy! You were meant for a general, and not for a dry goods clerk."

CHAPTER XVI.

FRANK IS DISCHARGED.

Frank Manton entered the office quite unconscious of the heavy accusation which had been brought against him.

"I saw Mr. Collins, Mr. Snobden," he said in a businesslike manner, "and gave him your message. He will call here tomorrow morning."

"Very well!" answered Mr. Snobden stiffly, for his suspicions had been aroused, as we know.

Frank turned to go out.

"Stop a minute!" said his employer. "I have something to say to you."

"Yes, sir?"

"Do you ever play poker?"

He scrutinized Frank's face as he spoke.

"No, sir," answered Frank much surprised. "Why do you ask?"

"Because I have been informed that you do."

"Whoever told you so has told you what is not true," said Frank warmly.

"Be careful how you try to deceive me. I cannot overlook deception," said Silas Snobden sternly.

"You won't have to in my case," said Frank, betraying no marks of guilt or confusion.

"Ha! perhaps I know more than you suppose. Read that letter!"

As he spoke he handed Frank the sheet of note paper which Gideon Chapin had put in his hands.

Frank read the letter with arched eyebrows.

"It seems to be written to you," continued his employer. "Of course there are other Franks, but the writer evidently alludes to your stepfather in his postscript."

"Mr. Snobden," said Frank, looking with his frank, honest eyes in his employer's face, "I have never seen this till now. I don't know what it means."

"You don't know what it means?"

"No, sir."

"Do you mean to say that you don't know Jimmy Keefe, the writer?"

"No, sir; the only Jimmy Keefe I know is a little boy three years of age. I don't think he wrote it," continued Frank with a smile.

"You know no other boy of that name?"

"No, sir."

"With whom do you play poker?"

"I never played poker in my life. I have heard of the game, but I can't play it. May I ask where you got this letter?"

"It was brought to me this morning."

"But if it was sent to me how could any one else get hold of it?"

"It was found on the floor of the warehouse—last evening. The presumption is, that you dropped it."

"Mr. Snobden," said Frank as a sudden suggestion came to him, "was it Mr. Gideon Chapin who handed you the letter?"

"Yes, but he did not find it. One of the junior clerks—John Higgins—found it."

"I begin to understand. It is a plot. Mr. Chapin is my enemy."

"What makes you think so? Because he brought this to me? It was only his duty. As he said, a poker player is not to be trusted."

"I dare say he is right, sir, but I am not a poker player."

"I should like to believe you, but circumstances are against you. I must believe you guilty. You may remain during the day, but tonight you can go. You will be paid up to the end of the week."

"But, Mr. Snobden, this is unjust. I can't help people writing letters, and pretending that they are for me."

"Possibly. If you can at any time prove your innocence I will take you back."

"I thought, sir, that one was considered innocent till proved to be guilty."

"That may be so in law, but I must follow a different rule. When I have reason to think that any one in my employ, boy or man, plays poker, or any other gambling game, he will receive his walking papers."

"Do you mind letting me keep the letter?" said Frank. "It may help me to prove my innocence."

"Here it is! It appears to belong to you, and I won't keep it from you."

"I have nothing to say except that I never saw it before. I will try to find out who wrote it, and why."

"Very well. You may now go to the post office. At the close of business you may call for your week's wages."

Frank bowed and left the office. His heart was sore, for he felt that he had fallen a victim to some one's malicious plot. He had little doubt that Gideon Chapin was at the bottom of it, and his suspicions were strengthened when he caught sight of Benson Tyler in the rear of the store in his company.

"I suppose he is to be my successor," he thought.

It was a heavy blow, but not so heavy as if he had no other income. The five dollars a week which he received from Allen Palmer would now be doubly welcome. Besides it might not be long, he hoped, before he obtained another business position which would occupy his days.

Gideon Chapin, while attending to his routine duties, had one eye on the office, which was separated from the main room only by a glass partition. He saw Mr. Snobden talking with Frank, then saw Frank leave the office looking unusually sober, and he guessed what had happened.

He rubbed his hands gently and smiled.

"It is working!" he muttered to himself. "It will all come right."

Five minutes later he went to the office.

"Excuse my intrusion, Mr. Snobden," he said apologetically, "but I am interested to know whether Frank Manton owns up to the letter."

"No, he denies that he ever saw it before."

"Dear, dear! how can he be so brazen?"

"Says he never played a game of poker in his life, and doesn't know the boy whose name is signed to the letter."

"Of course, of course! Very natural! But he mistook you, sir. He thought you were a man easily deceived. He thought he could pull the wool over your eyes."

"If he expects that he will find himself very much mistaken," said Mr. Snobden irritably.

"Of course he will. It is great presumption in him to think so lightly of you. Have you reduced his wages? It would be only reasonable."

"I have discharged him, Mr. Chapin. No boy or man who plays poker can work for me."

Gideon Chapin had expected this, but he was glad to be assured of it.

"I am glad of it. There is nothing like acting promptly in such a case. May I ask—ahem!—who is to succeed him?"

"You may send your nephew to me."

"I will, Mr. Snobden," said Gideon joyfully. "I shall be proud and happy to have him in your employ."

He lost no time in sending Benson to the office.

"Now look sharp, Benson. Be very respectful and deferential, and make him believe that you are a model boy."

"Your name?" asked Silas Snobden when the boy appeared in his presence.

"Benson Tyler."

"Your age?"

"Sixteen."

"Do you play poker?"

"No, sir," answered Benson. "I hope not. My uncle wouldn't let me."

"The other boy does. If I engage you to take his place do you think you can serve me faithfully?"

"I will try to, sir."

"Then you can report for duty tomorrow morning. I understand your uncle lives at your mother's house?"

"Yes, sir."

"You can come over with him then. Mind you are punctual. You will receive four dollars a week."

Benson's face fell.

"I—I thought the other boy got five," he ventured to say.

"So he did, but not at first. When you have been here long enough, if you are satisfactory, you will also receive five."

Benson was disappointed, but he was too prudent to show it to his new employer. He went back to tell his uncle that he had been engaged, and then left the store to return to Brooklyn.

At the corner of White Street and Broadway he met Frank. He smiled significantly, and stopped short.

"I hear you've been bounced," he said, with a triumphant smile.

"Yes—most unjustly," was Frank's quiet reply.

"Do you want me to tell Mr. Snobden that?" he asked.

"Yes, if you like. I told him so myself."

"I'm going to take your place."

"I expected it."

"Did you?"

"Yes, and I think I know who got up the plot against me."

"Who was it?"

"I don't think you need any information, nor your uncle either."

"Mr. Snobden asked me if I played poker, ho, ho!" laughed Benson.

"If you know anything about it, you know more than I do. I must leave you now, as I must report at the office. I hope you won't be discharged for nothing as I have been."

"He feels pretty well cut up," soliloquized Benson. "It is rather hard on him. Uncle Gid's a sharp man. He told me he'd get me the place, and he has."

CHAPTER XVII.

FORCING A LOAN.

"Well, mother, I'm discharged."

This Frank said to Mrs. Manton when he entered the house in the evening.

"Discharged?" repeated the poor lady in astonishment.

"Yes."

"What has happened?"

"An enemy has been plotting against me. He carried false tales to Mr. Snobden, and he believed them."

"Was it a boy?"

"No; it was one of the oldest employees of the house, who wanted the situation for his nephew. The scheme was very ingenious, and it succeeded."

"Who was this man?" asked his mother indignantly.

"Gideon Chapin. I don't think he ever liked me. Still, he wouldn't have done anything against me if he had not wanted a place for his nephew. Benson Tyler—that is his name—enters upon his duties tomorrow morning."

"Can there be such mean people in the world?" exclaimed Mrs. Manton.

"I am afraid there are plenty of them, but there are good people, too. Mr. Palmer is one of the kindest of friends, and little Rob, I really believe, loves me like a brother. He is a sweet little boy, but he is very delicate, and I know his father is very much afraid he will not live to grow up. If it were not for the five dollars a week I get from there, we should not know how to get along."

"If Mr. Palmer hears of your discharge, won't it hurt you in his estimation?"

"He will hear it from me, and I am sure he will take my part. Has Mr. Gerrish been here lately, mother?"

Frank could not make up his mind to speak of Luke Gerrish as his stepfather.

"He has not been here for a full week. I hope he has left the city, or got tired of persecuting us."

Mrs. Manton had scarcely finished speaking when the door opened, and the man of whom they were talking staggered in, and sank rather heavily into the nearest chair. He looked from one to the other, and seemed to enjoy the dismay which he read in their faces.

"Good evening, my dear; good evening, kid!" he said. "I'm quite a stranger, ain't I? I expect you missed me."

"We got along without you," answered Frank dryly.

"Oh, did you? Well, I couldn't get along without you. Nothing but business would keep me away from the wife of my bosom, eh, Mrs. G.?"

Mrs. Manton did not answer. The sight of this man filled her with loathing, and she asked herself, not for the first time, what could have induced her to marry him.

"Come, you don't seem sociable. Haven't you a word to say to me?"

"If you want some supper," said Mrs. Manton, in a constrained voice, "I will prepare some for you."

"Won't trouble you, my dear. I took supper with a friend of mine an hour ago. But there's something I do want, and that is money."

As he spoke he looked sharply at Frank.

"You have come to the wrong place for money, Mr. Gerrish," said the office boy quietly.

"Have I? Don't you earn four or five dollars a week at old Snobden's?"

"I did, but now I don't."

"Why, what's up?"

"Mr. Snobden has discharged me."

"I don't believe it," said Gerrish suspiciously. "You say this to get rid of giving me any money."

"I wish I did, but it's all true."

"What did he bounce you for? Have you been stealing?"

"No, sir; I am as honest—as you are!" answered Frank, with intentional sarcasm.

"Then why did he send you off?"

"Another boy wanted my place, or his uncle for him, and they got up a plot against me. They said I'd been playing poker, and Mr. Snobden believed it."

"Poker's a nice game, Frank. If I'd knowed you played poker, I'd introduce you to some friends of mine who've got money. I'll coach you a little, and you and I between us can clean them out."

"But I don't play poker," answered Frank in disgust. "I don't know anything about the game."

"You'll soon learn. I'll give you a lesson now;" and Gerrish produced from his pocket a greasy pack of cards.

"I don't care to learn, Mr. Gerrish. Besides, I've got an engagement for this evening."

"I'll go down tomorrow and see if the story's true about your being bounced," said Luke Gerrish, his suspicions returning.

"You can go if you like. I don't think Mr. Snobden will give you a very warm welcome. Your coming to the office before didn't do me any good."

Gerrish was at last obliged to believe that Frank had really lost his place. He looked rather glum, for he had depended upon raising a little money that evening.

"You got paid off, didn't you?" he asked suddenly.

"Yes."

"Then give me the money."

"Shame on you, Mr. Gerrish!" said Frank indignantly. "How do you think my mother and I are going to live?"

"If it comes to that, how am I going to live? That's what I want to know."

"Go to work. You are a strong, able bodied man, and you ought to be able to earn your living."

"Listen to me, Frank. I don't want you to *give* me money. I want you to lend me some, that is all. If you'll lend me two dollars, I've a good chance to get ten, or perhaps twenty tomorrow. Then I'll pay you up, I will, upon my word!"

"How are you going to make so much money in so short a time?"

"By betting on the races. I've got a straight tip for tomorrow. Why, a friend of mine won fifty dollars only yesterday. Just hand over two dollars, that's a good boy, and I'll give you back five if I win, I swear it."

"And if you don't win?"

"I'm sure to win with the tip I've got. It'll set me on my feet, and I'll buy a new dress for your mother if I'm very lucky."

"I don't believe in betting on horse races, Mr. Gerrish, and I know you are a good deal more likely to lose than win."

"You kids seem to know a good deal. Mrs. G., tell the boy to give me the money, or give it to me yourself if you've got it."

"I cannot oblige you, Mr. Gerrish. I think about betting just as Frank does."

Gerrish looked from one to the other with a glance of baffled fury.

"You'll hear from me," he said angrily. "That's a pretty way to treat a husband and father. Mrs. G., you are a heartless woman. You look calmly on and see me suffer, and won't reach out your hand to help me."

"My mother had a right to expect that you would support

her," said Frank. "Generally a man expects to support his family."

"And so I will, if you'll give me a chance. All I ask is the loan of two dollars, and I'll pay it back tomorrow night without fail."

"It is of no use, Mr. Gerrish. You won't get any money here."

"Won't I?" repeated Gerrish, an ugly look appearing on his face. "Then I'll have to help myself. That's all you've left for me to do."

He snatched a shawl from a chair on which Mrs. Manton had placed it, and said triumphantly, "I can get something on that anyhow."

"Oh, Mr. Gerrish, I can't spare that," pleaded Mrs. Manton. "I have no cloak, and that is my only safeguard against the cold."

"Can't help it, my dear. I'll send you the ticket, and you can redeem it tomorrow."

He was about to leave the room with the shawl, but Frank placed himself resolutely in his way.

"Put down that shawl!" exclaimed the boy with flashing eyes. "Have you got so low as to rob my mother of her clothing to gratify your taste for drink?"

"Get out of the way, kid, or you'll get hurt."

He raised his arm, and there seemed to be danger of a collision between Frank and his stepfather, in which the boy could hardly fail to have been seriously hurt.

"Let him have it, Frank!" exclaimed Mrs. Manton, much alarmed. "If he is unmanly enough to rob me of my only shawl let him do it."

"You hear what your mother says, kid! I don't want no trouble, but if you won't give me any money I must do the best I can."

"No," returned Frank, whose blood was up, "I won't let you carry off that shawl."

As he spoke he tried to snatch the shawl from his stepfather. The latter seized the boy by the collar, and Frank was in great danger of being badly hurt when a knock was heard at the door.

"Come in!" called Frank.

The door opened, and a tall, muscular young man appeared, holding a quart measure of milk in his hand.

"I say, what's up, Frank?" he said, looking from one to the other.

CHAPTER XVIII.

MR. GERRISH RETREATS IN DISORDER.

"You see," said Frank. "This man is trying to steal my mother's shawl."

"Let that boy alone, you thief!" said the young man sternly.

"Mind your own business, you loafer!" retorted Gerrish, sullenly.

"It is my business to protect this boy and his mother."

"Do you know who I am?"

"I know what you are. You are a thief."

"Do you want me to kill you?" demanded Luke Gerrish, frowning wrathfully.

"Did you hear me tell you to let go that boy?"

"I did, and I won't!" said Gerrish defiantly.

The milkman said nothing, but he wrenched Luke's hand from Frank, and faced him resolutely. Luke Gerrish was himself a strong man, but Seth Hastings possessed phenomenal strength. In his hands the ex-convict was like a child.

"I will have you arrested!" said Gerrish angrily. "That woman is my wife, and whatever is hers is mine. What have you got to say to that?"

"Is this true?" asked Hastings in surprise.

"He is my mother's second husband, I am ashamed to say."

"Why haven't I seen him before?"

"Because he has spent the last five years in Sing Sing, for burglary."

"You don't want him round, then?"

"No. He wants to live on us, and has been trying to extort money ever since he got back."

"Enough said! Get out of here! You're not wanted."

Luke Gerrish laughed contemptuously, and sat down in a chair, crossing his legs and staring defiantly in the face of the young man.

Seth Hastings was incensed, and resolved to teach the bully a lesson. He wasted no time in threats, but seized Gerrish by the collar, drew him out of the chair with irresistible force, kicked the door wide open and flung him down stairs.

"Excuse me, Mrs. Manton," he said, turning to Frank's mother. "I am sorry to have been obliged to use violence, but it is the only proper treatment for such a bully."

"Thank you, Mr. Hastings," said Frank warmly. "I only wish I had your muscle. I wouldn't let that man annoy my mother."

"Be cautious, Mr. Hastings," said Mrs. Manton anxiously. "Mr. Gerrish may be waiting for you outside."

"He won't if he knows what is best for himself. Good day!"

Seth Hastings went down stairs and found Gerrish on the sidewalk looking ugly.

"I'll get even with you for your impudence," he said. "I have a good mind to call a policeman."

"There is a good chance. Here is one coming."

Luke Gerrish gave one glance at the blue coated guardian of the city's peace, and walked quickly away. He always avoided an officer when he could. Between him and the police there was an irrepressible antagonism. Seth Hastings on the contrary waited till officer Woods came up.

"Do you see that man, Mr. Woods?" asked Seth, pointing to the retreating figure of Gerrish.

"Yes, Seth," answered the officer, who knew the milkman well.

"He's a convict who has just left Sing Sing. He has been

annoying Frank Manton and his mother. I caught him trying to steal a shawl from their room."

"Do you want to give him in charge?"

"Not now, but please keep an eye on him, as he may come round here another day. Will you know him again?"

"Small doubt of that, Seth. I'd remember that phiz among a thousand."

"I'll tell you a secret. He's Frank's stepfather, and is trying to live on him and his mother."

"I'll keep an eye on him," said officer Woods, nodding his head significantly. "It won't be safe for him to play any of his tricks in my precinct."

Luke Gerrish walked away disgusted.

"I'm in bad luck," he said. "If it wasn't for the name of it I'd be better off in prison. That woman appears to forget that I am her husband, whom she swore to love and cherish at the altar."

So perverse and one sided was his way of looking at things that he actually persuaded himself that he was an ill used man.

"And that kid," he resumed, "has thrown himself out of work just to spite me. If I could get him alone, I'd——"

He did not finish the sentence, but the ferocious expression on his face augured ill for Frank if he ever fell into his step-father's clutches.

An hour later Frank went to Mr. Palmer's to spend the evening with little Rob, as usual.

"Good evening, Frank," said the banker cordially. "Have you been hard at work today?"

"About as usual, sir. Tomorrow I shall be at leisure."

"How is that?"

"I have been discharged."

"Discharged!" repeated Mr. Palmer in astonishment. "Is Mr. Snobden dissatisfied with you?"

"I have an enemy in the store who has told him that I am in the habit of playing poker."

"It is untrue, of course?"

"Yes, sir. I don't know the game."

"Tell me the circumstances, and I may be able to advise you."

"I shall be glad to do so, Mr. Palmer."

Frank told the story of the letter, and the use made of it by Gideon Chapin.

"Do you think Mr. Chapin believes the charge he has made against you?"

"No, sir. He wished to get me out of the office in order to put his nephew in my place. His plans have succeeded, and Benson is my successor."

"That is certainly very mean. Who, do you think, wrote the letter?"

"A young clerk named John Higgins. He found it on the floor of the warehouse, so he says. I think Mr. Chapin arranged with him to write the letter."

"If you had the letter, you might have some chance of verifying your suspicion."

"I have the letter, sir."

"Let me see it."

Mr. Palmer examined the letter attentively.

"Do you know this young man's handwriting?" he asked.

"No, sir."

"Could you procure any for purposes of comparison?"

"I might write him a letter, sir, and ask for an answer."

"A good idea! Do so, and I will put it into the hands of an expert, and ask for his report. Write in such a way as not to excite suspicion."

"I think I can do it."

"Very well! That is the first thing to do. Meantime your income is reduced one half."

"Yes, sir; if my evenings were not employed, I don't know what I should do to get along."

"Until you get another place, I will give you eight dollars a week instead of five. Will that relieve you from embarrassment?"

"O yes, sir. You are very kind, Mr. Palmer," said Frank gratefully.

Allen Palmer smiled pleasantly.

"It is the least I can do in return for the prosperity which God has granted me. Do you or your mother owe any debts?"

"No, sir."

"That is well. Always avoid debt if you can. It is a hard task master. By the way, your suit is getting shabby."

Frank blushed with mortification.

"It is true, sir," he said. "I am saving up money for a new one. I know I do not look well enough to visit such a house as yours."

"My dear boy, that was not in my mind, I assure you. Yet I can see that you need to be better dressed. It will help you to obtain a place. I think a boy of your figure can easily be fitted with a ready made suit."

"Yes, sir. I bought this suit ready made."

"How long since?"

"A year ago."

"Naturally it is now too small for you. For twenty five dollars I think you can not only buy a suit but a hat and a pair of shoes. I will see if I have that sum about me."

The banker opened his pocket book, and drawing out two ten dollar bills and a five put them in Frank's hands.

"Thank you, sir. You are doing a great deal for me."

"You deserve it all. You have brought sunshine into the life of my little Rob. It is I who am under obligations."

He spoke with feeling, and Frank could see how deeply devoted he was to his little boy. He did not wonder, for he too had become warmly attached to Rob, whose warm heart and old fashioned ways gave him an unusual charm.

"I am going out this evening," said the banker, rising. "I don't like to go out so much, but my engagements are many. I am happy to think that I leave Rob a companion whose society he enjoys."

Frank had to tell the story of his dismissal over again to Rob whose sympathies were excited.

"What a wicked man Mr. Chapin must be!" he said.

"He is selfish at any rate, and unscrupulous," said Frank.

"Is his nephew a good boy?"

"He may be, but I don't like him."

"Perhaps Mr. Snobden will find out that you are innocent and take you back."

"I don't think I should care to go back to his office. He is not an agreeable man."

On Frank's way home, while walking past Reservoir Park, on Sixth Avenue, his foot came in contact with something on the sidewalk. He stooped over, and picked it up. To his surprise he found it to be a small portemonnaie. It was too dark to examine its contents, so he slipped it into his pocket and kept on his way home.

CHAPTER XIX.

IN SEARCH OF AN OWNER.

It was not until the next morning that Frank thought to open the portemonnaie. It proved to contain three dollars in bills, and some memoranda on a half sheet of note paper which had been folded up and placed in the pocket book. These memoranda were quite unintelligible to Frank and seemed to him of little value. But on the paper was a name and address, which was likely to be the name of the owner. It was:

SAMUEL GRAHAM.

No. 202 CLINTON PLACE.

"I will call there as soon as I have bought some new clothes," decided Frank. "The portemonnaie doesn't seem to be very valuable, but it ought to be restored to the owner."

Frank, after breakfast, walked down Broadway till he came to a large clothing emporium. He looked at the display in the windows, and finding the prices favorable he entered. The sum of money given him by Mr. Palmer went farther than he expected. He not only secured a very neat suit, but a hat, a necktie, a pair of shoes, and some underwear. He put on the new articles and requested to have the old ones sent home. As he left the store he came upon his successor Benson Tyler, who appeared to be walking up Broadway on an errand. Mr. Snobden's new office boy regarded Frank with astonishment. Yesterday he had been shabby. Today he was handsomely dressed.

"Are you working in there?" asked Benson, eying him curiously.

"No; I haven't any place yet."

"You seem to be all togged out."

"Yes," answered Frank with a smile, "I needed some new clothes."

"But I thought you were a poor boy?"

"I am sorry to say that you are correct."

"Then where did you get the money to buy *them* clothes?"

Benson ought to have spoken more grammatically, but he was careless.

"Even poor boys must get new clothes sometimes," replied Frank.

"But I don't understand. You are better dressed than I am."

"You have a place and I haven't."

"Oh, now I know how you got the money to buy new clothes," said Benson suddenly.

"How?"

"You won it playing poker."

"I never played poker in my life," returned Frank angrily.

"I don't believe you. That's why you were discharged."

"It was a story trumped up by your Uncle Gideon to get you into my place."

"Uncle Gid's a sharp man," said Benson complacently, "but I say, I wish you would teach me to play poker."

"Would you like to learn?"

"Yes."

"And get discharged as I was?"

"Oh, I'd take care old Snobden wouldn't find out."

"Or your uncle?"

"Oh, he wouldn't tell on me."

"You'll have to ask somebody who knows how to play, I don't."

"You're sharp!" said Benson. "I don't blame you. I don't see as it's any of old Snobden's business any way. But you might tell me. I wouldn't say a word."

"Then you really think I play poker?"

"To be sure I do."

"Then all I have to say is that you're mistaken. Where are you going?"

"To the Metropolitan Hotel with a message for a gentleman there."

"I advise you to go on then, for Mr. Snobden doesn't like to have his office boy loiter on the way."

"I shouldn't think you'd tell me that."

"Why not?"

"I should think you'd want to have me discharged as I have taken your place."

"I don't. I am sorry to lose the place, but I hope soon to have another. I don't care to go back to Mr. Snobden again."

"I wish I knew where he got them clothes," thought Benson. "He must have been playing poker last night with the wages he got paid. I'd like to join some poker club myself."

When Benson returned to the store he sought out his uncle.

"Who do you think I saw when I was out, Uncle Gid?"

"How can I tell?"

"That boy, Frank Manton."

"You saw him? How was he looking—down in the mouth?"

"Not much. He was togged out in new clothes, new shoes and a new hat. I tell you what, he looked like a dude."

"That is very surprising. He always said he was poor."

"He doesn't dress like a poor boy. Do you think he won the money at poker?"

"Perhaps so," but Mr. Chapin did not speak in a tone of conviction, for he knew very well that the charge against Frank was groundless.

"Has he got a new place?" asked the old clerk.

"He says he hasn't."

"He had better not refer to Mr. Snobden. It wouldn't do him much good."

It was fortunate for Frank that he had better friends than Gideon Chapin, who, as is usual, disliked the boy he had injured.

Frank was destined to another meeting, even less agreeable than the one with his successor. He had just passed Bleecker Street on his way up to Clinton Place when he encountered Luke Gerrish, who was walking arm in arm with one of his boon companions. His step was somewhat unsteady, and his face was flushed. He might have passed Frank without noticing him, but for a remark of his companion which led him to look up. As his eye fell upon Frank he clutched his companion's arm and halted in sheer astonishment.

"Well, if I ain't flabbergasted!" he ejaculated.

"What's the matter, Luke?" asked his companion.

"What's the matter? Look at that kid!"

"What of him?"

"Why, he's my precious stepson, he is, and dressed like a duke."

"Has he come into a fortin'?"

"Looks like it. Where did you get them clothes, kid?"

"I bought them, Mr. Gerrish."

"Ha! you bought them, and gave a good sum of money too. Think of that, Bolter, and last night he refused to give any money to his poor father? There's ingratitude for you!"

"Beastly ingratitude!" assented Bolter.

"And all the while he's rolling in money, positively rolling!"

"You are mistaken, Mr. Gerrish. I am poor, and have lost my position, as I told you."

"Looks likely, with them clothes!"

"They are a present to me from a gentleman who has been kind to me."

"Introduce me to the kind gentleman. Tell him I am your stepfather, who is down on his luck, and too sick to work."

"It wouldn't do any good, Mr. Gerrish."

"Listen to that, Bolter. He has no feeling for me, that boy. What have you done with your old clothes?"

"They are to be sent home."

"Then you've just bought them?"

"Yes."

"Where did you buy them?"

Luke Gerrish was crafty, and it occurred to him that he might call at the clothing store, and by misrepresentation obtain possession of Frank's old clothes and pawn them.

"It is not necessary to say, Mr. Gerrish."

Luke Gerrish might have insisted, but for a clever thought that came to him. Frank would probably put on the old clothes, the next day, and leave the new suit at home. This he might be able to secure, and it would command a considerably larger price than the old one. So he only said, "All right, kid! I'll get even with you yet."

"What do you say to a boy like that, Bolter?" he asked, as he pursued his unsteady way down town. "He has no more feeling for me than if he was a—ostirsch."

"Just so!" growled Bolter.

"But I'll get even with him yet, Bolter, see if I don't. He isn't a match for the old man, eh?"

"No, I should say not."

Frank soon reached Clinton Place, and was not long in finding the number of which he was in search.

He rang the bell at a modest brick house. The door was opened by the housemaid.

"I would like to see Mr. Graham," he said.

"Back room on the top floor," said the girl briskly.

"Is he a young man?"

"No; I thought you knew him. He's an old gentleman, with gray hair, what he's got left."

"Is he in his room now?"

"Yes; he stays there all day, writing."

"Writing?"

"Yes, he's writing a book, I believe."

"Do you know what kind of a book?"

"I guess it ain't a love story. He's too old and grumpy for that. Have you got business with him?"

"Yes, a little."

"You can go right up."

Frank's curiosity was somewhat excited by what he had heard. He went up three flights of stairs and knocked at the door of the rear room.

"Come in!" he heard from within.

He opened the door, and found himself in a small room with a bed in one corner. A plain wooden table was placed in the center of the apartment. It was covered with books and papers. Seated on a wooden chair beside it was a stout old gentleman, with a head like Horace Greeley, partly covered with scanty white hair. A soft broad brimmed hat hung on a nail above his head. He looked up as Frank entered, and surveyed him through his spectacles.

"Is this pocket book yours?" asked Frank, holding it in his hand, and extending it to the old gentleman.

CHAPTER XX.

FRANK OBTAINS A LITERARY
ENGAGEMENT.

"Yes," answered the old gentleman eagerly, in response to Frank's inquiry concerning the ownership of the pocket book. "It is mine. Where did you find it?"

"Near Reservoir Park on Sixth Avenue."

"My young friend," said Mr. Graham gratefully, "I am *deeply* indebted to you."

"You are quite welcome."

"He must be poor," thought Frank, "or he would not be so grateful for the return of three dollars."

"Probably," continued the old gentleman, "you thought the portemonnaie and its contents of small value."

"I did not think it very valuable unless there was more money than I found in it. I hope none is missing," he added with some anxiety.

"No; there were but three dollars. That is of little consequence. It is this paper which is of value," and he drew out the half sheet of note paper. "Does this surprise you?" he asked with a smile.

"I wouldn't give a nickel for it," admitted Frank.

"Probably not; but you will understand its value when I tell you that I am writing a history of the Saracens, and this paper contains reference to books in the Astor Library which I was three days in making. It represents three days' hard work."

"I begin to understand, Mr. Graham."

"I have always been a writer," continued the old gentleman, "but this is to be the great work of my life. It is upon this I depend for my reputation," he added, with a mild glow upon his venerable features. "I spare no pains, but the work is wearing, and I am sometimes in doubt whether I shall live to complete it. I am sixty nine years old."

Frank considered sixty nine a very great age, and he thought the old gentleman ought now to be released from work.

"How long have you been at work upon your book, sir?" he asked.

"Five years, and it is scarcely more than half done."

"Then at that rate you will be seventy four when it is completed."

"Yes," answered Graham with a sigh; "and who knows if I shall live till that age?"

"You look pretty healthy, sir," said Frank, wishing to cheer him up.

"True; and I come of a long lived family. My father lived till eighty one."

"I should think you would want to take life easier now that you are old."

"If I had no work—no interest in life—I should fret myself to death. No; I shall work to the end, or at least as long as I have health and strength."

"Then you find your work interesting?"

"Yes; but not all of it. There is copying to be done at the Astor Library, and a good deal of drudgery. I don't enjoy that, but it is necessary; yes, it is necessary."

"Do you work all day, sir?"

"Yes, as long as the light serves."

"Why don't you get some one to do the copying for you, sir?"

Graham's face lighted up.

"An admirable idea!" he said. "Why have I not thought of it before?"

"I don't think it would cost much, sir."

"I shouldn't mind that."

Frank was surprised. He glanced rapidly around him at the plain furniture and contracted room. Everything seemed to indicate poverty.

Mr. Graham smiled, for he read the thoughts of his young visitor.

"Confess now," he said. "You think me poor?"

"I thought you might be," stammered Frank.

"You judge from my plain surroundings. But I came here to be out of the way. When I lived up town in a fashionable street I was subject to constant interruptions, for I have a considerable acquaintance, and it seriously interfered with my work. Here no one calls to see me, and when I wish to see my friends I call upon them."

"I am glad you are not poor, sir. It is very inconvenient to be poor."

"Do you speak from experience, my young friend?"

"Yes, sir."

"I own a brown stone house up town which lets for three thousand dollars a year, and I have besides some investments in bank stocks."

"Then you are rich!" exclaimed Frank in surprise.

"I suppose I should be called so, at any rate when my simple mode of life is considered. Why, I spend less than a thousand dollars a year—considerably less, I think."

"I thought you might be dependent on your history for a living."

Mr. Graham broke into an amused laugh.

"My dear young friend," he said, "I should indeed be in poor case if I depended on my literary labors for support. I don't write for money, but for reputation. I want to be remembered after death," he concluded with enthusiasm.

"I am sure you will be, sir."

"Do you really think so? But of course you cannot judge. Still it may be," he added musingly, "if I live to finish my history."

As he spoke his glance fell on the portemonnaie. He opened it and took out the three dollars which it contained.

"Take it with my thanks," he said, extending it to Frank.

"But, sir, I don't want to be rewarded for my honesty."

"Then take the money as a mark of my friendship, my young friend."

"I will do that, sir, and thank you."

"You say you are poor. It will be of more service to you than to me. Are you attending school, or are you in a business position?"

"Neither, sir. I have been in a wholesale house down town, but I am not employed just now."

"Are you a good, plain writer?"

"Shall I give you a specimen of my handwriting?"

"If you please. Here is a sheet of paper."

Frank took a pen, and wrote a line or two. Mr. Graham examined it with satisfaction.

"Very well, very well indeed!" he said. "I am glad you don't indulge in any flourishes or fancy strokes. You write a plain, intelligible hand."

"I am glad you like it, sir."

"I believe you are the very assistant I want. I think you can help me materially, and abridge by a year or two the time needed to complete my history. Are you open to an offer of employment?"

"Yes, sir; I shall be very glad to be employed."

"Can you begin tomorrow morning?"

"Yes, sir."

"Then meet me at ten o'clock at the portal of the Astor Library. The works I want to consult are chiefly to be found there. Indeed that is the reason why I have selected a room in Clinton Place. Perhaps, as I am not poor, you are surprised to find me in an attic room."

"Yes, sir."

"I will tell you the reason. Being up so high I have no one over my head. I once had the room below, and this room was occupied by a young clerk who used to practice his dancing lessons over my head. You may suppose that it did not help me in my historical writing."

Frank laughed.

"I shouldn't think it would, sir."

"Your hours will be short. I shall never want you before ten o'clock in the morning, and I shall generally dismiss you at four in the afternoon—sometimes earlier, if there is not much to do."

"Those hours will be easy, sir."

"Now about the compensation? How much did you get in your last place?"

"Five dollars a week."

"Then I will give you six. The position of an historical assistant is more dignified than that of an office boy, and should be better paid. But there is one caution I must give you."

"Yes, sir."

"You will naturally be taken into my confidence. You will acquire a knowledge of the sources from which I draw my materials. You might be tempted to undertake a history of the Saracens on your own account."

Frank burst into a hearty laugh. The idea seemed to him irresistibly comical.

Mr. Graham laughed also, and rubbed his hands. Frank saw that he was indulging in a little joke at his expense.

"I will promise you faithfully not to get up a rival history, sir," he said.

"That relieves my mind very much," rejoined the old gentleman. "It has been done, let me tell you. I know of a literary man whose private secretary played this trick upon him. But I have your word," he added with a smile.

"Yes, sir; I shall keep it for more reasons than one."

"I think you will. Well, good morning. I will expect you tomorrow. Remember to be at the portal of the Astor Library at ten o'clock sharp. I will be in waiting, and instruct you in your duties."

As Frank left the house he said to himself, "I haven't had to wait long for a position, but I should never have dreamed of such an agreement as this. I wonder who the Saracens are, any way!"

CHAPTER XXI.

AT THE ASTOR LIBRARY.

As Frank entered the room about dinner time his mother said, "I hear that a boy is wanted at the druggist's round the corner. The wages are only four dollars a week, but that is better than nothing."

"I am not in the market, mother," returned Frank cheerfully. "I go to work tomorrow morning at six dollars a week."

"Indeed!" said Mrs. Manton joyfully. "What sort of place is it?"

"Writing history," answered Frank gravely.

"I suppose that is a joke."

"It is a very practical joke, mother. I am hired as assistant to a gentleman who is writing a history of the Saracens."

"But what assistance can a boy like you give?" asked his mother in surprise.

"I don't wonder you ask, mother. I will tell you all about it."

"You are certainly fortunate," said Mrs. Manton when Frank had finished his story. "I hope you will give satisfaction to your employer."

"Who knows but I may become a historian myself, mother? I have heard of 'The Boy Detective' and 'The Boy Actor.' Why not 'The Boy Historian'?"

"There are other lines in which boys are more likely to excel," said Mrs. Manton sensibly.

The next day Frank presented himself in front of the Astor

Library a few minutes before the hour specified. Soon Mr. Graham came shuffling up.

"Ah, you are here, my young assistant," he said well pleased. "Let us go in."

When they entered the main library room, Mr. Graham directed him to seat himself at a table, and going up to the desk left orders for certain books which he brought himself and laid before Frank with half a dozen sheets of foolscap. Opening the volumes he indicated certain passages which he wished copied.

"When your work is done, return the books, and come to my study," he said.

Then he shuffled out of the library and betook himself in haste to his elevated room.

Now it chanced that on that particular morning the library was visited by a party of English gentlemen to whom one of the librarians acted as guide, answering their questions courteously.

"Who principally patronizes your library?" asked Sir Ralph Moulton, who was one of the visitors.

"Scholars and literary men," was the answer. "It is a treasury of information to those who are preparing works on special subjects. More than one valuable work has been written from materials obtained here."

Looking about, Sir Ralph discovered Frank writing busily at a table.

"Is that one of your American authors?" he asked with an incredulous smile.

"I don't know. He is a new figure here."

"May I ask him?"

"If you like."

"Ahem, young man, are you engaged on any literary work?" asked Sir Ralph. "Excuse my—ahem!—curiosity."

"Certainly, sir," answered Frank in a matter of fact tone. "I am gathering material for a 'History of the Saracens.'"

"Most astonishing!" ejaculated the baronet, opening his eyes wide in amazement. "May I inquire your age?"

"I am sixteen, sir."

"How very remarkable! You are the youngest author I have ever met. Is the work well under way?"

"Yes, sir; it is nearly half done."

This information Frank had obtained from Mr. Graham. "And how long do you think it will be before it is completed?"

"Probably three or four years."

"I am amazed at such precocity. I would be glad to subscribe for a copy."

"If you will give me your address, sir, I will let you know when the work is finished."

"There is my card. Will you favor me with your autograph?"

"With pleasure, sir."

Frank wrote his name on a card handed him by Sir Ralph, and the baronet put it carefully in his pocket.

"You Americans are a very remarkable people," said Sir Ralph. "In England we have few historians under forty."

When Frank told Mr. Graham of his interview with the English baronet the old gentleman was much amused.

"At any rate," he said, "you have probably secured me a purchaser of my history. I am especially pleased that it should be an English gentleman of position. I think I must in my preface give you credit for the literary assistance you have rendered me."

"Thank you, sir, that would make me very proud."

Mr. Graham beamed upon him benevolently through his spectacles.

"That shows me that you believe in me as an historian. I earnestly hope that the book may deserve the compliment. Did you find the task I assigned you very dry?"

"On the contrary sir, I became very much interested in it."

"That is well! I am glad to have my collaborator interested in his work."

As a matter of fact Frank did become interested in the task assigned him. Though he did not even know who the Saracens were when he commenced his work, he soon became very well informed about them, and Mr. Graham delighted to talk with him on his pet subject, finding in Frank an intelligent listener. The boy secretary even ventured upon an occasional suggestion which sometimes struck the historian favorably.

Frank's handwriting was very plain, and this was an important matter to Mr. Graham, whose eyesight was defective. On Saturday night, though the week was incomplete, Mr. Graham handed him six dollars.

"But, sir, I have only worked three days," said Frank.

"That doesn't matter. I am so well pleased with having obtained your services that I am willing to pay the extra amount."

"Do you find that I have really helped you, Mr. Graham?"

"I think I shall accomplish at least a third more through your assistance," said the historian. "Moreover, the work you do in copying was most distasteful to me, and I looked upon it in the light of drudgery. I am only afraid you will get tired of the company of an old man, and will seek some more congenial employment."

"You need not be afraid of that, sir. I am gaining information every day, and my hours are easy."

Frank had been about two weeks in his new place when late one afternoon, while walking on Broadway, he met John Higgins, the clerk who had found the letter which had been used against him so effectively by Gideon Chapin.

Higgins half stopped, as if with the intention of speaking to Frank, but his manner betrayed doubt and indecision.

Frank took the initiative.

"How are you, John?" he said.

"Tip top," answered Higgins eagerly. "I—I hope you are well."

"I'm all right, thank you!"

"Have you—got a place?" asked Higgins with some anxiety.

"Yes; I got one the day after I left Mr. Snobden."

"I am glad to hear it," and there was something in his tone that showed he was sincere.

"Look here, John," said Frank, "I am glad to meet you, because I have a question to ask you."

"I am—in a little of a hurry," returned Higgins, evidently confused.

"Then I will go along with you and not detain you. My question is this: where did you find that letter Mr. Chapin showed Mr. Snobden?"

"On the floor," said Higgins, looking down.

"Where?"

"I—I don't remember exactly where."

"Do you think the letter was one that I dropped?" asked Frank, pointedly.

"I suppose so, as it was addressed to you. It looks like it, don't it?"

"Yes, it looks like it; but the first I ever saw of the letter was when it was shown me in Mr. Snobden's office."

"That's queer!"

"Yes, it is queer," returned Frank in an emphatic tone.

"I don't know anything more about it than that I picked it up on the floor."

"Why did you give it to Mr. Chapin? Why didn't you give it to me if you thought it was mine?"

"I—I don't exactly know. Oh, yes; Mr. Chapin saw it in my hand and asked me what it was. Then he took it from me. That is how it happened," continued Higgins, in a tone of relief, for he thought the explanation a plausible one.

"*Are you sure you didn't write it yourself?*" asked Frank, fixing his eyes intently on the face of his companion.

CHAPTER XXII.

THE NEW OFFICE BOY.

"I don't understand you," stammered John Higgins, flushing and looking painfully embarrassed.

"I think you do," said Frank significantly. "Do you remember receiving a letter a week since inviting you to become a member of an athletic club?"

"Yes."

"You answered it?"

"Yes. I said I would join. I haven't heard anything more about it."

"I wrote the letter."

"You did! It was signed by another man."

"That is true. The letter was a decoy letter."

"A what?"

"A decoy letter. There is no such club."

"Then why did you write it?"

"I wanted a specimen of your handwriting. Well, I have compared it with the letter that got me into trouble, and I have made a discovery. Would you like to know what it is?"

John Higgins did not answer, but scanned Frank's face with a troubled look.

"I have discovered that you wrote the letter which you say you found. Why did you do this? Did you want to get me into trouble?"

"No," answered Higgins earnestly.

"Then why did you write it?"

"I—I don't like to tell."

"Then I will make a guess. Mr. Chapin asked you to do it."

As Frank spoke he watched the face of his companion closely.

"How did you find out?" asked John Higgins in a confused tone.

Of course this was tantamount to a confession.

"Because I knew that he disliked me and wanted my place for his nephew. But I can't understand why you should consent to help him."

"I couldn't help it," said Higgins desperately.

"Why couldn't you help it?"

"Because he threatened to get me into trouble if I didn't do as he required. Now you know all about it."

"I see that it was a very mean trick."

"But I couldn't help it. You see that for yourself?"

"No, I don't. I wouldn't have written such a letter to be used against you, no matter what Mr. Chapin threatened."

"I didn't want to do it, Frank, for I always liked you, but I suppose I am a coward, and old Chapin forced me into it. I suppose I ought to be ashamed of it."

"I think you ought."

"What are you going to do about it? Are you going to Mr. Snobden to tell him? If you do I'll get discharged."

"I haven't made up my mind yet what I will do. I don't care to go back into Mr. Snobden's employment. I like my present place better. I get six dollars a week where I am. Till within a week of the time I left, Mr. Snobden only paid me four."

"I am glad you have a better place," said John Higgins, sincerely.

"What I want you to do is this. We will go into a hotel, and I want you to write on the letter that got me into trouble a statement that it was written by you by Mr. Chapin's orders."

"I—don't think I would like to do that."

"Then do you want me to carry these two letters to the office, and show Mr. Snobden?"

"No, no! I'll do as you say."

"Then come in here."

They were near the Sturtevant House. Frank led the way into the writing room on the left hand side of the entrance, and signed to John Higgins to follow him. The room was at that time unoccupied. Frank directed Higgins to sit down at the table, and then dictated the following sentence.

This letter was written by me at the request of Mr. Gideon Chapin, and was never seen by Frank Manton until it had been put into the hands of Mr. Snobden. I did pick it up from the floor of the warehouse, but I had previously dropped it there. I solemnly declare that this is a true statement.

JOHN HIGGINS.

"What are you going to do with the letter?" asked Higgins anxiously.

"I shall keep it by me for the present. I want to have it in my power to disprove the charge made against me, if it is ever likely to be repeated."

"Then you won't show it to Mr. Snobden at present?"

"No."

John Higgins seemed relieved by this assurance.

"How do you like the new office boy, my successor?" asked Frank.

"I don't like him at all."

"What is the matter with him?"

"He's very disagreeable—puts on no end of airs. Just because Mr. Chapin is his uncle he thinks he is a person of great consequence."

"How does Mr. Snobden appear to like him?"

"I don't think he likes him much. I have heard him speak harshly to him. When Benson goes out on an errand he always stays a long time, and that Mr. Snobden doesn't like. One of the clerks heard him say the other day, 'I wish I had Frank Manton back. He's worth a dozen of this boy.'"

Frank's face showed the gratification he felt.

"I suppose you could go back if you went to Mr. Snobden."

"I don't want to go back, but I am glad he is beginning to appreciate me," said Frank. "The fact is, I was very unjustly treated, and although it has done no harm, I can't help feeling it."

"I wish you were back again. I like you much better than the new boy. You won't think hard of me because I wrote that letter, Frank?"

"I will forgive you, John, but I hope you will never do such a mean act again."

It was as Higgins had said, Mr. Snobden began to suspect that he had made a bad bargain when he exchanged Frank Manton for Benson Tyler. He was not long in discovering that the new office boy was untrustworthy, and ready to shirk work whenever he could conveniently do so. He felt that he would have been glad to have Frank back again, even if he did play poker, but he did not know where he lived.

"Mr. Chapin," he said one day, "do you know where Frank Manton lives?"

"No, sir; why do you ask?" inquired Gideon, in alarm.

"I begin to think I made a mistake in discharging him."

"But, sir, think of employing an office boy who plays poker!"

"He did not remain away so long when sent on an errand as your nephew does."

"Benson does not play poker."

"That may all be true without making him a good office boy."

"I will speak to him, Mr. Snobden. Leave it to me."

"Do so. I am getting dissatisfied with him, and unless he turns over a new leaf I must find another office boy."

When they were on their way to Brooklyn that evening Mr. Chapin called Benson to account.

"Do you know that you are in danger of losing your place, Benson?" he asked.

"It isn't much of a place," grumbled Benson. "I only get four dollars a week."

"If you want to be raised you must please Mr. Snobden."

"What does old Snobden say about me?"

"He says you stay away too long when sent on errands."

"A fellow can't run all the time. He expects too much for four dollars a week."

"There are plenty of boys who would be glad to step into your shoes."

"Tell Mr. Snobden that if he will pay me five dollars a week, instead of four, I will do all I can to please him."

"If I gave him such a message it would do you no good. Try to please him first, and higher wages may come soon."

"I don't believe they will. He's too mean."

"Be careful how you speak in that way of your employer, or he may send for Frank Manton again."

"Frank Manton won't come if he does send for him."

"How do you know that?"

"John Higgins met him the other day. He has a handsome new suit, and is earning six dollars a week in a new place."

"You don't say so!" ejaculated Gideon Chapin, not over pleased with the news.

"Yes, and he says he doesn't want to come back. Now do you wonder, Uncle Gideon, that I am dissatisfied with four dollars a week when Frank Manton earns six?"

"It is too bad, I admit, but be patient for a short time and I will see if I can't get you an advance."

"I hope you will, Uncle Gid, for I find it hard work to get along."

Two weeks passed, and to Mr. Chapin's surprise Benson did

not again broach the subject of higher pay. At the same time he seemed to be better supplied with money than usual. But one day Mr. Snobden called his bookkeeper into the office.

"Mr. Chapin," he said, "I want to consult you about a little matter. *I find my stock of postage stamps is diminishing very fast. There must be a leak somewhere.*"

"Are you sure of this?" asked the bookkeeper, with a troubled look.

"Yes. I have made a little estimate, and I think some one is abstracting from two to three dollars' worth every week."

CHAPTER XXIII.

A BOY DETECTIVE.

"I hope you don't suspect me of taking the stamps," said the bookkeeper anxiously.

"No, Mr. Hale. Such a thought has never entered my mind."

"Thank you, sir," said the young man with a gratified look. "You know I have free access to the office, and I thought——"

"I know very well you have the opportunity," said Mr. Snobden, who though not an agreeable man was disposed to be just, "but I made up my mind about you a good while since."

"Have you any suspicions as to the guilty party, sir?"

"There is another person who has free access to the office, and is sometimes here alone."

"You mean the office boy?"

"Yes, I mean Benson."

"I don't like the boy, but I should be sorry to think that he would take what did not belong to him. Is he not related to Mr. Chapin?"

"Yes, he is Mr. Chapin's nephew."

"Have you spoken to Mr. Chapin about the matter?"

"No, and I don't intend to at present. He would make it known to the boy and put him on his guard. My idea is, to have Benson followed and watched so that we may, if he is guilty, catch him in the act of selling the stamps."

"A good idea, sir."

"How would a telegraph boy do?"

"He might attract Benson's attention and excite his suspicions."

"True, and the same would be the case if any person in my employ was delegated to the office. Have you any suggestions to make?"

"Yes, sir. Near the corner of White Street I have often observed a bright, wide awake boy who makes a good living by shining shoes. I know him somewhat, having from time to time employed him. If you wish I will set him on Benson's track. The office boy would never suspect that he was watched."

"Your plan is a good one. Will you see the boy, and make a satisfactory arrangement with him? I leave all to your discretion."

The bookkeeper made it convenient during his dinner hour to walk round the corner of Broadway. There stood Tom Holt, a boy of fifteen with his shoe box over his shoulder. He wore a slouch hat and a business suit considerably the worse for wear. He had large eyes, and a bright, intelligent face.

"Shine, sir?" he asked.

"I don't mind," said the bookkeeper. "How is trade today?"

"Might be better, sir."

"Do you like the business?"

"No, sir; I want to get out of it, but I can't afford to give it up till I get something better."

"How would you like to be a detective?" asked Mr. Hale smiling.

"First class, but no one would employ a boy like me."

"Not permanently perhaps, but I have a little job in which you can help me."

"I'm your man," said Tom eagerly. "What is it? Do you think I can do it?"

"It is very simple. Do you know of Snobden and Downs, in White Street?"

"Yes, sir."

"Do you know the boy who works there as office boy?"

"I don't know him. I have seen him."

"That will answer. Do you think you could follow him without his noticing it?"

"Well, I should smile. I shouldn't be any sort of a detective if I couldn't. What's up about him?"

"He is suspected of taking stamps from the office and disposing of them. I want you to follow him, and see if he goes into any place where stamps are bought."

"Yes, sir, I know them places."

"I hope you have never dealt in them."

"No, sir, I don't do that kind of business. I'll have to be poorer'n I am now before I take to stealing."

"That is good. What is your name?"

"Tom Holt."

"Very well, Tom. Keep on the watch tomorrow morning and all day until you have found out whether my suspicions are correct."

"All right, sir."

The next morning a strip of fifty two cent stamps was left ostentatiously on Mr. Snobden's desk. The bookkeeper quitted the office for a few minutes, and it was arranged that Benson should be sent in for a letter which had been left on the desk.

Benson's eye fell immediately on the postage stamps. Another office boy with whom he had formed a casual acquaintance had put him up to this method of adding to his income. When he first appropriated a few stamps, it was with fear and trembling, but the theft, so far as he knew, was not discovered, and the sum he realized from the sale supplied him with a little spending money. Of course he tried it again. Such a large number of stamps was used in the office that, as he flattered himself, the disappearance of a few would not be noticed. So nearly every day he managed to abstract a few, for which

he found a ready sale at a penny each in a small shop not far
from Wall Street.

When he saw the strip of fifty stamps his eyes glistened. He
looked cautiously about him to see whether he was observed.
Deciding that no one was watching him, he tore off thirty of
the stamps, slipped them in the side pocket of his sack coat,
took the letter, and went out. The letter was not to be mailed,
but was for personal delivery.

The bookkeeper glanced at Benson as he came out of the office.

"Have you the letter?" he asked carelessly.

"Yes, sir."

"Very well, you may take it at once to the address."

"Am I to wait for an answer, sir?"

"You may inquire if there is any answer."

"All right, sir," replied Benson with unusual cheerfulness.

After he left the store the bookkeeper entered the office, and
examined the stamps.

"He has taken thirty," he said. "It is just as I thought. The
young rascal only took part, hoping to elude suspicion. With
the help of my young detective I shall soon find out what he
does with them."

Benson walked briskly up the street and hurried into Broadway. Generally he loitered on his errands for the firm but now
he made more haste, in order to get time to attend to his own
commission. It happened, and this too had been arranged by
the bookkeeper, that the letter was directed to a person whose
place of business was in the immediate neighborhood of the
party who bought stamps. Benson thought he might as well
attend to his own business first, and accordingly went at once
to the dealer in stamps.

It never occurred to him to notice the boy with a blacking
box hung over his shoulder who followed him at an easy gait,
keeping perhaps twenty feet distant.

"I wonder whether he's got any stamps," thought Tom. "If he ain't I'll have my walk for nothing."

Tom followed Benson down Broadway, but at the corner of Chambers Street he had a slight detention.

"Here, boy, give me a shine," said a stout, gray haired gentleman.

Generally Tom would have been glad to accommodate a customer, but now it threatened to defeat his more important business.

"Thank you, sir," he said, "but I'm sent on an errand and cannot stop now."

"It will only take you five minutes."

"I cannot afford even that time, sir. Very sorry."

"You are the most disobliging boy I ever met," said the old gentleman angrily. "I will never employ you again."

"Very sorry, sir, but there's another boy. Here, Johnny," beckoning to a boy on the opposite side of the street, "here's a gentleman wants a shine."

Benson was nearly two hundred feet in advance, but Tom quickened his pace, and caught up with him. It was his first appearance in the role of the "Boy Detective," and he liked it.

Benson hurried into Nassau Street, and Tom followed him.

Not far from Broad Street Benson halted, and turning down a side street entered a small shop. He was so intent upon his errand that he did not observe that he was followed in by a bootblack.

"Here are thirty stamps," said Benson, in a business-like tone, laying them on the counter.

Without a word the man on the other side took the stamps and laid down three dimes.

These Benson took and pocketed with an air of satisfaction. Turning he caught sight for the first time of the boy detective. Tom drew out ten stamps with which he had been provided by Mr. Hale, and laid them down on the counter.

A dime was shoved out to him, and he left the shop immediately after Benson.

"Where did you get your stamps?" asked Benson, rather surprised that a bootblack should have anything of the kind to dispose of.

"A man give 'em to me," answered Tom.

"I suppose so," remarked Benson with a knowing smile.

Tom Holt winked. "I see it ain't no use to humbug you," he said. "If I was a office boy I could get more," he added, "but I don't take many in my business."

"Maybe I could get you to sell some for me—on commission. Where do you hang out? Haven't I seen you on Broadway, near White Street?"

"Yes, I am around there 'most every day."

"All right! I'll see you again."

"You may see me once too often," thought Tom.

CHAPTER XXIV.

A CHANGE IN THE OFFICE.

Nothing was said to Benson that day about the stamps, and he left the office under the impression that his pilfering had not been discovered. By arrangement Mr. Hale remained after office hours, and reported to Mr. Snobden what he had discovered.

Silas Snobden was very angry.

"I don't mind the loss of the stamps," he said, "so much as the treachery of the boy. I would rather have given him twice the amount he realized for them than have had this happen."

"He isn't the boy that Frank Manton was."

"I begin to think that I made a mistake when I discharged him. Still, playing poker is a serious matter."

"From whom did the information come? He denied it."

"It was Gideon Chapin who showed me the letter written to him from one of his fellow gamblers."

"Mr. Chapin wanted to get Frank's place for his nephew, did he not?" remarked the bookkeeper significantly.

"What do you mean to hint?" said Mr. Snobden quickly.

"Only this: that the letter was trumped up to injure Frank with you."

"Do you think Mr. Chapin had a hand in it?"

"I think it not impossible."

Silas Snobden was silent. He was not an agreeable man, but he aimed to be just.

"If I thought that," he said, "I would send for Frank and reinstate him. As to Mr. Chapin, I would give him distinctly to understand that one more such trick would lose him his place."

"I met Frank Manton three days since. He has a good place with a better salary, and would not care to return."

"Have you any boy you can recommend, Mr. Hale?"

"Yes, I think well of the boy Tom Holt whom I employed to follow Benson. He is sharp and intelligent, and as to honesty I would agree to stand responsible for him."

"I should like to see him."

"He is just outside. I told him to be on hand as you might like to question him."

"Can you call him in?"

Mr. Hale went to the door and called Tom who entered rather bashfully with his blacking box over his shoulder.

"Tom," said the bookkeeper, "this is Mr. Snobden."

Tom bowed respectfully.

"I have seen you often, sir," he said.

"What is your name?" asked the merchant.

"Tom Holt."

"Have you parents?"

"No, sir, I am an orphan."

"Where do you live?"

"At the Newsboys' Lodge."

"How would you like to give up your present business, and become an office boy?"

"Very much, sir," answered Tom, his eyes glistening.

"Mr. Hale here speaks well of you. He thinks you will be faithful and honest."

"Thank you, Mr. Hale," said Tom gratefully. "I will take care to deserve your recommendation."

"The boy will need some new clothes," said Mr. Snobden, surveying Tom's professional costume critically. "I may be fastidious, but I shouldn't like to have my office boy wearing a vest with only one button."

"I can give him an outfit," said the bookkeeper. "I am a small man, not more than an inch taller than Tom. I have a suit and underclothing which I can spare him."

"Then that removes one difficulty. How much ought I to pay him?"

"I am afraid he would find it difficult to get along on four dollars, as he has no home. If you could pay him five——"

"I will pay him six," said Silas Snobden, considerably to the surprise of his bookkeeper. "I have made up my mind that it is better to pay a boy a living salary than have him help himself."

"You are very kind, sir," said Tom earnestly, "and you too, Mr. Hale."

Mr. Snobden regarded Tom with unusual kindness. It was clear that he was favorably impressed with his appearance.

"You may come tomorrow morning at nine o'clock," he said. "Mr. Hale, will you see that he is presentable?"

The bookkeeper invited Tom to accompany him home and spend the night. There he provided him with a complete outfit, which altered the boy's appearance very much for the better.

It was not until an hour after Benson's arrival that Tom presented himself at the door of Snobden & Downs.

As he entered the store, Benson, who happened to be standing near the door, regarded him with surprise and curiosity.

"Hallo, where'd you get them clothes?" he asked.

"A friend gave them to me."

"Did you call to see me? Just wait till I go out on an errand."

"No. Mr. Hale asked me to call."

"What have you to do with Mr. Hale? Do you know him?"

"Yes."

Just then the bookkeeper came up.

"Benson," he said, "Mr. Snobden would like to see you in the office. Tom, you may remain here for the present."

Still Benson suspected nothing. When he entered the office

he saw his uncle, Gideon Chapin, standing beside Mr. Snobden's desk.

"What is up?" he asked himself a little uneasily.

"Mr. Chapin," said Silas Snobden, clearing his throat, "have you any reason to doubt the honesty of your nephew?"

"Certainly not," said Chapin with emphasis.

"I have discovered during the last week that I am being systematically robbed of postage stamps."

"I hope you don't suspect Benson," said Gideon Chapin.

"Look at his face!" said Mr. Snobden quietly.

Benson's face was a vivid red. He seemed overwhelmed by the charge.

"Benson," said his uncle sharply, "have you taken any postage stamps from the office?"

"No," answered Benson faintly.

"You see the boy denies it," said his uncle. "Who has charged him with theft?"

"Mr. Hale."

Gideon Chapin regarded the bookkeeper scornfully.

"I don't want to insinuate anything," he said, "but the bookkeeper has just as much chance to steal stamps as the office boy."

"What have you to say to this, Mr. Hale?" asked Silas Snobden.

"That it is true. Still, I submit that when the office boy can be proved to have sold stamps to a dealer, it looks suspicious."

"Who says he has done so?"

"Excuse me a moment."

Mr. Hale opened the door of the office and called "Tom."

Tom Holt entered, and stood respectfully waiting to be questioned.

"Do you know that boy?" pointing out Benson.

"Yes, sir."

"Did you follow him yesterday when he left the office at one o'clock?"

"Yes, sir."

"Where did he go?"

"To a dealer in stamps near Wall Street."

"What did he do there?"

"He sold thirty two cent stamps for thirty cents."

"Did you see him do it?"

"Yes, sir."

"You sold some stamps yourself," said Benson with flaming face.

"That is true. I sold ten for ten cents."

"Then what have you got to say against me? You did the same thing. You told me a man gave them to you."

"What man gave them to you?" demanded Gideon Chapin sharply.

"Mr. Hale."

"Ha!" exclaimed Chapin significantly. "Just as I thought;" and he regarded the bookkeeper with malicious satisfaction. Mr. Hale, however, did not seem in the least disturbed.

"I authorized him to do what he did," remarked Silas Snobden quietly.

"I see. There is a plot against my poor nephew," said Gideon bitterly.

"Mr. Chapin," said his employer, "let me caution you not to make such accusations. I have reason to believe that there was a conspiracy against Frank Manton, designed to create a vacancy for your nephew, and that you were implicated. I will not, however, investigate the matter unless you make it necessary for me to do so."

Gideon Chapin looked the picture of embarrassment. He saw that he was discovered, and maintained a prudent silence.

"Benson, you are discharged!" said his employer. "If you will accompany Mr. Hale to the cashier's desk you will receive wages to the end of the week. Let me advise you in future to resist temptation if you wish to get on in the world."

Benson left the office with hanging head.

"You miserable young fool!" hissed his uncle, who went out at the same time. "You have disgraced yourself. I wash my hands of you. You will get no help from me hereafter."

The boy could not command a word in reply. He began to feel that he had made a terrible mistake. Even the bookkeeper pitied him.

"Benson," he said kindly, "you are young, and this, I presume, is your first fault. You can redeem yourself."

"If Mr. Snobden will only take me back I will never steal again."

"He won't do that, but you can get another place where you can show yourself worthy. You will make friends if you deserve them."

"I will try to do so," said Benson, touched by the unexpected kindness.

"You may go to the post office, Tom," said Mr. Snobden to his new office boy. "I hope it won't take you as long as it did Benson."

CHAPTER XXV.

LITTLE ROB TAKES A WALK
WITH FRANK.

Frank continued his evening attendance at the house of Mr. Palmer. Little Rob's affection for him was very strong, and this was regarded with much satisfaction by the banker.

"You seem to have given my little boy a new interest in life, Frank," he said pleasantly one Saturday evening.

"I am very glad of that, sir. I am very fond of Rob. He seems like a brother to me."

"Most boys of your age would find it wearisome to spend so much time with a little boy."

"It is the pleasantest part of the day to me, Mr. Palmer."

"Do you like it better than writing the 'History of the Saracens'?" asked the banker jocosely.

"Yes, sir; though I find that interesting too."

"Do you know what Rob asked me last evening after you went away?"

"Perhaps to have me discharged," said Frank with a smile.

"No, indeed! That would break his heart. He says I ought to raise your pay to seven dollars a week."

"But, sir, my time can't possibly be worth that."

"I think it is to Rob and me. You make him happy, and that is worth a great deal to me. I have decided to accept his suggestion. Let me begin this evening, by paying you the increased amount."

"You are very kind, sir, and the money is very welcome. I have long been wanting to buy my mother a new dress, and have waited till I could buy a nice one."

"You are evidently a good son. Now for another matter. I find that I must start for Chicago tomorrow evening to be absent a week at least. The business is of importance, and I cannot well put it off, but I am troubled about leaving Rob in the house alone. Could you arrange to stay here while I am gone, making it your home in fact?"

"Yes, sir, if Mr. Graham can spare me."

"Perhaps he can get along with half his usual time. You might stay with him till one o'clock, and then ride up town and lunch here with Rob. Of course you can relinquish half your salary as I shall pay you fourteen dollars a week instead of seven while I am away."

"I feel sure he will consent, as he does not seem to be hurried in his work."

"Then I may consider that settled, and will tell Rob of my journey."

Little Rob seemed quite satisfied when told that Frank would be with him during the afternoon and at night.

"We'll have great fun," he said. "Will you go out to the Park with me every pleasant afternoon?"

"Yes, Rob. I will go anywhere you like."

"Then I am afraid you won't miss me at all, Rob," said his father.

"Yes, I will. I love you *bestest*, but I love Frank too."

"I am very glad you do. I am sure there is room enough in your heart for both."

"You are my papa, but Frank seems to me like a big brother." Mr. Palmer smiled.

"Rob is bound to get you into the family," he said.

When on Monday morning Frank broached to Mr. Graham

his plan of curtailing his hours of work for a week or more, the historian readily assented.

"I can spare you very well," he said. "I have considerable material on hand, and shall not require new citations for the present."

"Then, sir, if you won't be inconvenienced I shall be glad to keep my promise to Mr. Palmer."

"Your time seems to be quite fully occupied. Are you acting as private tutor to the banker's son?"

"No, sir; Rob is delicate, and needs me rather as a companion than a tutor."

"Perhaps Mr. Palmer will buy a copy of my History when it is completed?"

"I think he will, sir."

"I should like to have his name among my subscribers. If you think the little boy would be interested you may bring him here to see me."

"I will, sir; but I didn't know you liked children."

"I like them if they are well behaved."

"I suppose you are not married, sir?"

"No, I have never found time. I may marry when my History is finished," he added reflectively.

As Mr. Graham was already nearly seventy there seemed some chance that he would be too old before his literary task was completed. Though he sincerely liked the old man, Frank, as he regarded his wrinkled face and scanty gray locks, was inclined to laugh, but forebore.

On Tuesday afternoon, finding that little Rob was in favor of the visit, Frank called on the historian with his young charge. The old fashioned boy regarded him with curiosity.

"Do you write histories?" he asked gravely.

"Yes, my dear boy, I am writing one."

"Frank told me about it. Doesn't it make your head ache?"

"Sometimes, but I can leave off work at any time."

"What a funny room this is! Are you poor?"

"No," answered Mr. Graham with a smile, "I have all the money I need, and more too."

"Then what makes you live up so high, right under the roof?"

"Because I can be quiet here."

"Does your wife live here too?"

"I have no wife. Do you think I am too old to marry?"

"I don't know," answered Rob thoughtfully. "I have read about some men in the Bible who married after they were a hundred."

The historian seemed very much amused.

"Then I shan't give up all hope," he said, his eyes twinkling through his glasses. "Perhaps you will buy a copy of my History when it is finished."

"I shall if I am alive," answered little Rob gravely.

Mr. Graham eyed Rob with some curiosity.

"Don't you expect to live to grow up?" he asked.

"Perhaps you don't know that I am very delicate," said Rob calmly. "I expect there's something the matter with my heart."

"You mustn't worry about that," said the historian.

"Oh, I don't worry about it. I have always heard that Heaven is a nicer place than the earth. But I should be sorry to leave papa and Frank."

"My dear child," said the historian nervously, "pray don't talk so. I don't like to hear about death. It isn't—cheerful."

"You are just like papa. He doesn't want me to talk about dying. Still if I was an old man like you, I should think of it a little."

"I am not so very old. I am only sixty five. I had an uncle live to eighty."

"I hope you'll live to finish your history. I wonder whether you'll meet any of the Saracens in Heaven."

"What a very strange idea!" murmured the historian.

"I suppose some of the Saracens were good. You would like to meet good Saracens, wouldn't you?"

17. "Why, he's dressed like a duke."

18. "Is this your pocket book?" asked Frank.

21. Higgins sat down
wrote at Frank's dicta

22. Tom Holt, the bootblack.

19. Mr. Graham soon made his appearance.

20. "How very remarkable! You are the youngest author I ever met."

23. "I wonder whether you'll meet any of the Saracens in heaven?"

24. "Ah, my lad, it's a cruel world for the poor."

"I don't think I should care very much about it."

"Did you ever see a Saracen?"

"No, my boy."

"Then I don't see why you want to write about them."

"Really, you are a most extraordinary boy!"

"Am I? Perhaps that is because I am delicate. Sarah—that's the girl that does the chamberwork—says I have queer ideas. She says it makes her creep all over sometimes to hear me talk. I wonder," continued Rob thoughtfully, "how it feels to creep all over."

"I don't know, my boy. I never felt that way. But I think Sarah is right about your having queer ideas."

Soon after Frank and Rob took their departure.

"Well, Rob, what do you think of Mr. Graham?" asked Frank.

"He seems a nice man, but he isn't handsome. I suppose he can write history just as well as if he were."

"I don't think that will make much difference, Rob. Where would you like to go next?"

"Suppose we go up to Madison Square and sit down on a bench."

"Do you feel able to walk so far?"

"Oh yes; I am feeling quite well and strong today."

As the boys walked up Broadway a man was coming through Fourteenth Street, and noticed them with interest and surprise. He was a rough looking man, and in appearance and manner suggested a tramp.

Not to keep the reader in the dark, it was Luke Gerrish. He had never heard of Frank's engagement at the banker's, and therefore was unable to account for his stepson's having in charge a young man who evidently belonged to a wealthy family.

"Who's that kid Frank's got in tow?" he asked himself. "How'd he come to know him anyway. Looks like a young swell. Maybe he's a lost boy, and Frank's goin' to restore him to his anxious parents and pocket a reward. If that's so I'll take a hand and claim half."

Luke followed the two boys at a cautious distance, and saw them take seats in the Square.

He established himself on a neighboring settee and set himself to watching them closely. Finally Rob espied him.

"Oh, Frank," he said, "there's a wicked looking man that's watching us all the time. I am afraid of him. Let us go."

Frank turned his glance in the direction indicated, and recognized his stepfather.

CHAPTER XXVI.

LUKE GERRISH MAKES A DISCOVERY.

Frank was far from pleased to see Luke Gerrish. He did not wish him to discover his evening engagement, and thus far had kept it from him. But now discovery seemed inevitable. It occurred to him that he might board the Broadway cars, and so elude his stepfather. But it was too late.

When Gerrish saw that Frank had recognized him, he rose from his seat and advanced to the bench where he and Rob were seated.

"Halloa, Frank?" he said with annoying familiarity. "Where are you going? I haven't seen you for an age."

"Do you know the man?" asked Frank, very much surprised.

"Yes, Rob," Frank answered in a low voice. "It is my stepfather, the man I have told you about."

"Oh! I don't wonder you don't like him."

"Come, Frank," proceeded Luke, "you ain't sociable. Who's that young nob you've got with you?"

"Why does he call me a nob?" asked the little boy.

"It's a young friend of mine," said Frank coldly.

"How do you do, my boy?" said Luke Gerrish, with an ingratiatory smile. "Won't you shake hands?"

"I—I think I'd rather not," said Rob.

"Why not?" demanded Gerrish with a frown.

"Because your hands aren't clean, sir," answered Rob nervously.

Luke Gerrish looked angry at first, but he quickly changed to a whining tone.

"You are right, my dear child," he said with a sigh. "I'm sensible of it, but I'm in hard luck, and them that ought to help me and stand by me have gone back on me. Ah, my lad, it's a cruel world for the poor."

"Are you very poor, sir?"

"Yes, yes indeed I am. The boy that's with you is my stepson. He and his mother live in comfort, but I am left out in the cold," and Luke wiped away an imaginary tear with a greasy coat sleeve.

"Why don't you work, sir?" asked Rob.

"Oh, my dear, I would gladly work, but I cannot find employment."

"My papa gave you a chance to get in some coal, but you didn't come to the house."

"Ah! are you the son of that kind gentleman? I forgot where he lived, and that's why I didn't come."

Little Rob gave him the correct address before Frank could prevent him.

"And does Frank come to see you often?" he asked.

"Why—don't you know?—he spends every evening with me. My father hired him to come."

"How long has he been going up to your house, my dear? He never told me of it."

"Three or four weeks, I believe."

"How very nice!" said Gerrish in a significant tone. "I wonder you didn't tell me, Frank?"

"I didn't want you to know, Mr. Gerrish," said Frank bluntly.

"You see how he treats me, my dear!" said Gerrish with another imaginary tear wiped away with his coat sleeve.

"Frank is a good boy. You mustn't say anything against him," said little Rob.

"He is good to you, I have no doubt, but he isn't good to me."

"He says you have been in prison."

"Oh, he said that, did he?" returned Luke, with a malignant glance. "He likes to talk against me."

"But it's true, isn't it?"

"Yes, my dear, it is true. But I'm an innocent man. A wicked man whom I trusted got me into trouble, and swore a crime upon me which he had himself committed. I spent some sad years in that terrible place—Sing Sing—and in all the time I never had a word of kindness or comfort from that boy or his mother. Now that I am released, they will have nothing to say to me. Last night I had to walk the streets, for I had not money enough to pay for a bed."

Rob was kind hearted, and though Luke's appearance made him shudder he could not help feeling pity for him.

"I have a quarter, Frank," he said. "May I give it to him?"

"If you like, Rob."

"Here, poor man, here is a quarter. I hope you won't spend it for drink."

"No, my dear, I won't. I am a strict temperance man. I shall go to a restaurant and buy a good meal. I have had nothing to eat for twenty four hours. I am not so good a man as your good father, but I am very unfortunate."

"You look strong and able to work."

"So I do, but my health ain't what it looks to be. I've got a fatal disease. My liver's almost gone, and the doctor tells me I'm liable to drop dead any moment from heart disease."

"What an accomplished liar!" thought Frank.

"Rob," said he, "if you are not too tired we will be walking home."

"I am a little tired, Frank."

"Then we will take the cars. Good afternoon, Mr. Gerrish."

"May I go with you, Frank?"

"Papa is not at home. He has gone to Chicago," said Rob.

"Has he now?" asked Gerrish with interest. "And how long is he going to stay?"

"About a week. I should be very lonely, only Frank stays with me nights, and all the afternoons, as well as evening."

"Seems to me you've got a soft snap, Frank," said his stepfather.

"What's that, Frank?" asked Rob, whose knowledge of slang terms was limited.

"He means that it is a good chance for me, Rob."

"And for me, too, Frank. I should be awfully lonely without you."

"Your pa must think a good deal of you, my dear."

"Yes, he does."

"And—are you an only child?"

"Yes."

Luke's eyes glittered with satisfaction. Evidently some idea had been suddenly formed in his mind. Whatever it might be, it boded no good to the little boy whose indiscreet confidence had suggested it. Frank became uneasy, fearing he knew not what. He was anxious to get rid of his stepfather of whom he was not only ashamed, but afraid, knowing his capacity for evil.

"Come, Rob," he said abruptly. "We will get on the cars. If we are going to Central Park we shall want to get there in good time."

"Good by, my dear," said Luke. "You haven't told me your name yet."

"You didn't ask me. My name is Rob Palmer."

"Well, good by. I hope I'll see you again."

Rob, under ordinary circumstances, would have reciprocated the hope, but he was a boy of truth, and he really did not wish to see Mr. Gerrish again.

So he only said gravely, "Thank you, sir."

Luke Gerrish stood on Broadway looking after the car which contained the two boys.

"I didn't know Frank was so sly," he said to himself. "He's got a soft snap, and had it for weeks, and he never let me know about it, nor did his mother either. I wonder how much he gets. As the boy's an only child it's likely he gets a good salary—maybe five dollars a week. Why, he must be making as much as ten dollars a week, and hands it all in to his mother. And I'm left out in the cold. If ever a man was ill treated I'm the one. Here's my wife and son livin' in luxury, and I'm obliged to go hungry, and sometimes do without a bed! It's shameful, so it is! I'm glad I've found it all out. It was lucky for me that I run across the two kids, or I might never have known how I was treated. Now I must consider what advantage I can get out of it."

Luke Gerrish was destined to another surprise, and to another unexpected meeting, for as he turned to walk down Broadway, he nearly came into collision with a young man, already mentioned in the earlier chapters.

"Why, John Carter!" he exclaimed. "How came you in the city? When did you arrive?"

"I got in this morning."

"And where have you been?"

"Philadelphia."

"Isn't it a little imprudent for you to come here so soon after——"

"That affair of my uncle's, I suppose you mean."

"Yes, that is what I mean."

"He's all right, isn't he? He won't trouble himself to look for me. In fact, he won't learn I am in the city, unless you tell that boy of yours."

"Frank is no longer Mr. Snobden's office boy."

"How is that?"

"He has been bounced."

"Humph! that is well. Do you think he will get another place?"

"He has got two already."

"I don't understand you, Luke."

"He has one place by day, and another in the evening. Why, he makes ten dollars a week, Jack."

"He's a smart boy. I congratulate you, Gerrish."

"What for?"

"Because it gives you better pickings."

"Jack," said Gerrish in the tone of one who is seriously wronged, "I haven't received a cent from the young imp since I came to New York, except a quarter which he once gave to get rid of me."

"That's queer."

"It's wrong—it's outrageous!" said Luke Gerrish forcibly. "That boy and his mother make no more account of me than if I was a stone. I didn't know till today that he had an evening job. Oh, he's a foxy kid!"

"So it appears. What is his evening job?"

"He has been engaged by an up town banker—Mr. Palmer— to keep his boy company. He's staying at the house now, while the father is in Chicago."

"How did you find that out?"

"I saw the pair of them in Madison Square. Frank wouldn't tell me anything, but I got the boy to talking. Carter, he's an only child, and his father dotes upon him. Don't you think—" here his voice sank to a whisper, and an earnest conversation ensued, the purport of which will appear hereafter.

CHAPTER XXVII.

LUKE GERRISH HAS A BRILLIANT IDEA.

About ten o'clock the next morning Luke Gerrish found his way to the residence of Allen Palmer, and rang the bell of the basement door.

A maid servant answered the summons.

She eyed Luke with a suspicious glance, for he looked very much like a tramp, and his face was far from prepossessing.

"Well, sir?" she demanded sharply, "what do you want?"

"My dear young lady," began Luke.

"I am not your dear young lady," returned the girl in an uncompromising tone.

"No, more's the pity. I could not expect such a handsome girl as you would say anything to me."

Katy was accessible to flattery, and she spoke more gently.

"If that's all you've got to say, you are only wasting time."

"I am sure you must have a charitable heart. When I tell you I have had no breakfast, I think you will relieve my hunger."

"Can't you get work?"

"I am expecting to go to work next Monday, if I don't starve before that time."

"You can come into the kitchen. I think the cook will find something for you."

Luke Gerrish followed her into the kitchen, where some bread and butter and cold meat were placed before him.

"I saw a beautiful little boy come out of the house one day," he said between two mouthfuls. "Does he live here?"

"He must mean little Rob," said the cook.

"Yes, I heard some one call him by that name. He looks like a sweet child."

"And so he is," said Katy, regarding Gerrish with much more favor than at first. "Do you like children?"

"I dote on them, miss. I only wish I had a child like little Rob."

"I'm afraid he wouldn't fare very well. You don't seem able to support yourself."

"True, true!" said Gerrish, wiping away an imaginary tear. "But I would work for him more than for myself."

"Then you have no children?"

"No, none of my own. I have a stepson, but he treats me badly. Because I am unfortunate and cannot work——"

"But why can't you work?"

"I have just come out of the hospital. I was there for six months—a case of chronic rheumatism. Why, miss, I couldn't move in bed without screaming, I was in such pain. I went to the house where my wife lived, but she and her son would not let me in. Oh, they have hard hearts."

Meanwhile Gerrish, who really had had no breakfast, did ample justice to the food that was set before him. He managed in a way that did not excite suspicion, to ask questions about the house and its arrangements, the answers to which, with the object he had in view, were likely to prove valuable to him.

After eating a hearty meal he rose to go.

"I am deeply obliged to you," he said. "You have saved my life."

"How is that?" asked Katy incredulously.

"Ah, miss, you don't know what it is to be near starvation. If you had refused me I was going down to the North River and throw myself in."

"You wouldn't do that?" said Katy with a shudder.

"Indeed, I would. Fate is against me. If when I was a young man, I had met a girl like you——"

"Oh, go along!" said Katy blushing. "As if I would marry you! Besides, you've got a wife."

"So I have, to my sorrow! I have a wife who breaks cups and saucers over my head when she is angry."

"And what do you do?"

"I—well, you wouldn't have me raise my hand against a woman, would you?"

"You don't look like a man that would stand still while his wife was breaking cups and saucers over his head."

"No, I don't look it, Katy—that's your name, isn't it? I was once a gentleman. I walked through the streets in—in Pough-keepsie, when I was twenty five, dressed in the height of fash-ion; more than one beautiful girl would turn back and cast admiring glances at me. But now, alas! all is changed. My wife has ruined my life."

"Perhaps she would have a different story to tell."

"She would, I have no doubt. She is always reviling me. But there are some good people in the world. Katy, I shall never for-get you. A thousand thanks!" and with a melodramatic gesture he walked down the block.

"What were you talking about with that man, Katy?" asked the cook.

"He was telling me about his troubles. He said his wife breaks cups and saucers over his head."

"I don't believe a word of it."

"I think it's true. Why, the tears came to his eyes when he told me of it."

"Katy, I think that man's a humbug. I hope he ain't up to any harm. Did you see how his eyes were wandering round while he was eating?"

"You are too suspicious, Sarah. He said he used to be a gentleman."

"It must have been a good many years ago."

Later in the afternoon Luke joined his friend, John Carter, in a saloon near the river, and reported progress.

"Can anything be done there, Luke?" asked Carter.

"I don't know. I should like to have gone up stairs, but there was no chance. I asked all the questions I dared, but I didn't want to excite suspicion."

"Allen Palmer is a very rich man," said Carter thoughtfully. "I have heard him rated at a million dollars."

"Very likely, but I'll tell you of something that he values more than all his stocks and bonds."

"What is that?"

"His boy," answered Luke.

"Does he value him more than you value your stepson?" asked Carter with a smile.

"That boy!" muttered Gerrish with a frown. "I'd like to choke him."

"You're a model father, or rather stepfather."

"Oh, drop that! Let us keep to business."

"What is the business before the house?"

"How to get some money out of Palmer."

"Well, what's your plan?"

"Did you ever hear of Charlie Ross?" asked Gerrish significantly.

"The Philadelphia boy who was stolen and held for ransom? I see—but isn't it dangerous?"

"There is no gain without some little risk. Why, Carter, we shall be playing for a big stake. Say Palmer is worth half a million dollars—he is worth that, isn't he?"

"Well, not far from it, I expect."

"Wouldn't he be willing to pay a hundred thousand for his only boy?"

"If he couldn't get him back in any other way."

"He wouldn't be willing to wait for that. We could let him

think the boy was sick, and worrying for home. That would bring him to terms."

Carter was silent for a moment.

"I don't half like the job, Gerrish," he said.

"Don't you think it will pay, or are you afraid?"

"Partly both; but it will be rather hard on the poor boy to take him away from home to such a place as we should keep him in."

"Have you joined the church, Jack?" asked Luke Gerrish with a sneer.

"I am more fit for it than you, Gerrish. You're a rascal through and through."

"Thank you, Jack," answered Gerrish in a mocking tone. "Considering how virtuous you are, I am afraid I am not fit company for you. Still, I never went so far as to hit my uncle on the head, taking the opportunity to rob him as he lay senseless on the floor."

John Carter flushed and looked embarrassed.

Gerrish was quick to take advantage of the point he had scored, and resumed:

"The fact is, Carter, we ain't either of us angels. You'll be a fool to give up such a promising job. Of course we won't hurt the kid. Come, will you help me? Remember, there's money in it."

"And I am reduced to five dollars. I must get money in some way."

"Then it's a bargain, is it?"

"I am with you, Luke."

A conference ensued, in which the details of the enterprise were agreed upon.

CHAPTER XXVIII.

LITTLE ROB IS SPIRITED AWAY.

As a general rule Frank did not reach the house of the banker till one o'clock. During the forenoon, therefore, little Rob was left to his own resources. He was allowed to go out into the street, but was forbidden to leave the block. However, he could go anywhere in the street between Fifth and Sixth Avenues. That there should be any danger to him within these restricted limits no one could imagine.

It was about ten o'clock on Saturday morning that Rob was standing near the corner of Sixth Avenue, when a young man came up to him hurriedly.

"Are you the son of Mr. Palmer, the banker?" he inquired.

"Yes, sir, I am little Rob Palmer," answered Rob in surprise.

"I thought so from your father's description."

"Do you know my father?"

"I have only recently made his acquaintance," answered John Carter, for it was he.

"My father is in Chicago."

"I know he went there, but I have bad news for you."

"Bad news!" repeated Rob, turning pale. "What is it?"

"Your father has met with an accident, and broken his leg."

"Is this true?" asked Rob wildly.

"Yes; and he has sent me to bring you to his bedside. He is in a good deal of pain, but he says that if he had his little Rob with him he would not mind so much."

"Where is he? Take me to him," said little Rob, the tears coming to his eyes.

"That is what I am going to do. I meant to bring a carriage for you, but there was no time. Come to Sixth Avenue, and we will get on the cars."

"Let me go back to the house and leave word where I am going."

This would not have comported with Carter's plans, and he said hurriedly: "There is no time for that. I will let you telegraph to them."

"But they will be anxious about me."

"Your papa told me to bring you back with me as soon as possible. You don't know how he is suffering."

To little Rob, with his affectionate heart, this was irresistible.

"All right!" he said with a sigh. "I will go."

He placed his hand confidingly in Carter's, and the two boarded a Sixth Avenue car.

"Don't say a word about your father in the car!" cautioned John Carter.

Little Rob did not understand the reason of this, but he was a little boy, and not suspicious, so he acquiesced.

With his quaint, old fashioned look he attracted attention in the car, and a benevolent looking lady beside him tried to start a conversation. Carter felt that this was dangerous, so he remarked quietly: "The little boy has heard some bad news, and doesn't feel like talking, ma'am."

"Indeed! poor dear!" said the lady compassionately. "Sorrow has come to him early."

"So it has, ma'am. Sorrow comes to all of us."

"No; but I am acquainted with his father, who has sent for him to come to his sick bed."

The lady, who was curious as well as sympathetic, asked two or three more questions, but Carter answered evasively.

At the other end of the car, on the opposite side, sat a rough looking man, red faced and unkempt, who watched Carter and little Rob closely.

It was Luke Gerrish, the fellow conspirator, who had remained in the background while his more respectable looking partner lured Rob into the trap which had been so artfully prepared for him.

"We will get out here, Rob," said Carter, in the neighborhood of Christopher Street.

"Is papa here?" asked Rob.

"He is not far away," answered Carter evasively.

"But I don't see why he should come here. It is not a nice place."

"No, but when he broke his leg he could not be carried far. The house where he was carried is not a nice one, but the people are kind and will take good care of him till he's able to be moved home."

"Will that be soon?"

"As soon as the doctor gives permission. You won't mind stopping in a poor house?"

"Not if my papa is there. But you will telegraph to the girls?"

"Yes, give me the name, and I will attend to it as soon as I have taken you to your father."

"The cook's name is Sarah Moriarty. I think you had better telegraph to her. She has been in the family ever since I was born."

"Sarah Moriarty," repeated Carter, ostentatiously writing down the name on a business card which he had in his pocket. "She will hear from you within an hour."

"I am glad of that, or she might get frightened. Ask her to send Frank here this afternoon."

"Who is Frank?"

"Frank Manton. He is a boy that keeps me company in the afternoon and evening."

"All right! I'll attend to it," and Carter noted down Frank's name.

"Frank Manton is about the last person I would send for," he soliloquized. "However, the boy will be none the wiser."

Little Rob, who was not observing, did not notice that the rough looking man at the end of the car followed them out, and continued to follow them down the side street into which they turned. As he had seen Luke Gerrish once in Madison Square, this might have excited his suspicions, but he was too much occupied with thoughts of his father to take any notice of his fellow passengers.

They finally stopped before a shabby looking house not far from the river, and Carter, still holding Rob by the hand, ascended the steps.

"Is my papa here?" asked Rob.

"Yes, I told you it was not a nice house. In a day or two your father can be moved to his own home."

"That will be much better."

The door was opened by a slatternly looking maid servant about sixteen years of age, who eyed Rob with curiosity.

"Is the room ready?" asked Carter.

"Yes, sir."

"Then I'll go right up. Come along, Rob."

Rob followed gladly, rejoiced that he was so soon to see his father. A door was opened on the second landing, and Carter drew him in.

Little Rob looked about him eagerly, but the room was unoccupied. There was a bed in the corner, but there was no sick man reclining on it.

"My father is not here," said Rob in bewilderment.

"No, my dear, he is not here," answered Carter with a smile.

"But you said he was here."

"I must have been mistaken. But here's a gentleman that will be a father to you."

As he spoke Luke Gerrish walked into the room and threw himself into a chair with his legs stretched out.

"Do you know me, little kid?" he asked.

"I'm not a kid," returned Rob indignantly.

"Oh, I forgot; it's only poor boys who are kids. Do you know me?"

"Yes, I do. You are a bad man. You are Frank's stepfather."

"Correct the first time! Does Frank say I am a bad man?"

"Indeed he does. He says you have been in prison," answered Rob.

"Does he now? Wait till I get hold of him!" returned Luke, with an ugly look on his face. "I'll show him whether I am a bad man or not."

"Why did you bring me here?" asked little Rob, turning to Carter. "Hasn't my papa broken his leg?"

"No, your papa's leg is just as sound as ever," replied Gerrish, with perfect coolness.

"I am glad of that," said Rob, looking very much relieved. "I want you to take me right home. There's no reason for my staying here."

"Sorry, my dear," said Gerrish with a grin, "but we couldn't do it just now."

"You have no right to keep me here," said Rob indignantly.

"Maybe not."

"My papa will have you both punished."

"Will he now? How is he going to find out where you are, or who took you away?"

Little Rob with difficulty stifled a sob. Life with him had always been smooth and peaceful. He had been reared in an atmosphere of affection and the wind had never blown upon him roughly. This was a new and startling experience to him.

"Why do you want to keep me here?" he asked.

"For the pleasure of your company," answered Gerrish mockingly.

"I don't believe you. You don't like children," declared Rob.

"Don't I? How do you know?"

"From your looks."

"Well, kid, you are not far wrong. Children in general are nuisances. But I may as well tell you why we nabbed you. We are very poor, and we are going to keep you here till your papa comes down with a big sum of money. You won't get hurt, so you needn't take on, but you've got to stay here till your father come to our terms."

"I understand," said Rob gravely.

CHAPTER XXIX.

MR. PALMER'S TELEGRAM.

Frank reached Mr. Palmer's house at one o'clock, his usual time. Of course he had no suspicion that anything was wrong. But when the door was opened he saw at once from the agitated look of the servant that something had happened.

"Have you seen anything of Rob?" she asked.

"No; isn't he in the house?"

"He went out on the sidewalk at about half past nine, for an hour, and has not been seen since. Cook and I are in dreadful trouble for fear something has happened."

"You have not seen him for three hours and a half!" ejaculated Frank, turning pale with apprehension.

"No. When he did not come in at the usual time I went out and searched for him all through the block, but he was nowhere to be found."

"He wouldn't stray away out of curiosity, to see something or other, would he?"

"No; his papa always told him he wasn't to leave the block, and he always obeyed him. Oh! I am afraid something terrible has happened to the poor little dear," and Katy wiped her eyes with her apron.

"I wish I had got here sooner," said Frank. "You are perfectly sure he isn't in the house anywhere?"

"Perfectly sure. Cook and I have searched the house from attic to cellar. It'll be terrible news to his poor pa, who is expected home tonight. He'll be blaming cook and me."

"I don't see how you are to blame. I will go down the block and see what I can find out."

Frank felt very much troubled, for he had become warmly attached to little Rob, and the uncertainty increased his anxiety. It was hard to tell what to do or where to inquire, but near the corner of the block on Sixth Avenue was a grocery store at which Mr. Palmer dealt. Frank had been in there with little Rob, so that those employed there were familiar with his personal appearance.

"If Rob left the block and went on Sixth Avenue," he said to himself, "he may have been seen by some one in the store."

As he reached the store a boy of fifteen—a young German boy named Charles Schaefer—came out with a basket of eggs which he was to carry to some customer.

"How are you, Charlie?" said Frank. "Have you seen anything of little Rob this morning?"

"Yes," assented the boy.

"How long since?" asked Frank eagerly.

"I saw him about ten o'clock."

"Where?"

"He was just turning into the avenue."

"Was he alone?"

"No; there was a man with him. Rob held his hand."

"Was it a rough looking man, about forty five, rather stout?" asked Frank, thinking of Luke Gerrish.

"No," answered Charlie, shaking his head. "The man wasn't more than thirty. His face was very red, like a man that drinks. He had red hair."

Frank started in surprise. The description reminded him of John Carter. But Carter, he had reason to believe, was out of the city, and likely to remain out, on account of his assault upon Mr. Snobden. Besides, how should he know anything of little Rob, and his connection with him?

"Where did they go?" he inquired anxiously.

"They got on a Sixth Avenue car, and went down town," answered Charlie readily.

"And you saw no more of them?"

"No."

"Thank you, Charlie, your information may be valuable."

It was a clew, but there was much more to find out.

"I wonder if Carter has been seen prowling round the house," thought Fred. "I will go back and inquire."

He went in at the basement door, and told what he had heard.

Katy and the cook were very much excited.

"Poor Rob has been stolen!" exclaimed the cook, bursting into tears.

"We must recover him," said Frank resolutely. "Tell me, has there any man with red face and red hair been here, or have you seen him anywhere near the house?"

The two girls exchanged looks.

"There was a man here yesterday," said Sarah, "a regular tramp he was, and he looked fifty if he was a day, but he had black hair."

"Did he come into the house?" asked Frank eagerly, for he suspected it was Luke Gerrish. "What did he say?"

"He talked about Rob, said he was a little angel, and he wished he had such a son. He said he had a wife and son who treated him very bad, and wouldn't let him come into the house, though he was sick, and had only just come from the hospital."

Frank's face lighted up. Here was a clew indeed!

"Go on!" he said.

"We gave him something to eat, and he seemed very thankful."

"Did he have a scar on his left cheek?"

"I don't know. I can't seem to remember," said Katy.

"Yes, he did," said the cook. "I took notice of it as soon as he came in."

"I know the man," said Frank quietly.

"Is he—a good man?"

"He is a very bad man. I am sure that it was he who planned the carrying off of little Rob."

"You don't mean it? Why you might knock me down with a feather!" ejaculated the cook.

As she weighed nearly two hundred, it would have taken a very large feather to upset her.

"And to think," she continued indignantly, "that we gave him a good breakfast, and then he ups and goes off with little Rob. I'd like to get at him," and she flourished a rolling pin in a way that might have brought terror to the soul of any man, even one as athletic as Luke Gerrish.

"The man who took him was a friend of this man. He didn't dare to appear himself. He would have frightened Rob by his looks."

"What will they do with him, do you think?" asked Sarah nervously.

"They won't hurt him. They have taken him to get money out of his father."

"What a wicked shame! But Mr. Palmer will give any amount to get back little Rob."

"He won't give a cent if I can help it," said Frank resolutely. "Now that I know who have taken him, I feel sure I can defeat their plans."

"And you are sure little Rob won't be murdered? I was in the house when he was born, poor little dear! I should die if anything happened to him."

"Don't be afraid! Luke Gerrish will be sick of his job before he gets through."

As Mr. Palmer was absent from home Frank felt an additional responsibility laid upon him. The servants were helpless and bewildered, and no assistance could be expected from them.

"I shall notify the police authorities," he said, "as I shall want all the help I can get."

"Yes, yes, you know just what to do," said Sarah. Young as Frank was, she felt that she could safely depend upon him.

He snatched a hasty lunch, for he did not know how long he might be absent. Just as he was leaving the house, a Western Union Telegraph boy came up the steps.

"Have you a message for any one here?" asked Frank hopefully. He thought the telegram might contain some news of little Rob.

"Does Frank Manton live here?" asked the messenger.

"I am Frank Manton."

"Then sign for the telegram."

Frank did so, and tore the envelope open.

This was the message he read. It was dated at Chicago.

I am detained here longer than I expected. I am afraid I shall not reach home till Tuesday. Stay with Rob if you can any way manage it.

ALLEN PALMER.

Fred read this telegram with mingled feelings. Upon the whole he was glad to think Mr. Palmer might possibly be saved the knowledge of Rob's abduction until the danger was over and he was restored to his home. He was unable to answer the dispatch, for he did not know at what hotel Mr. Palmer was staying, and no address was given in the message.

"My responsibility is all the greater," he said to himself. "Now, Frank Manton, you must do your best to justify Mr. Palmer's confidence and find little Rob."

Informing the servants of the telegram he had received Frank went at once to notify the police of what had occurred.

"Can you describe these men?" asked the sergeant. "My men must be able to identify them."

"There are two officers who will know them by sight."

"Who are they?"

"Officer Snow and officer Grubb."

"I will assign them to this job. Be here in an hour and give them all the information in your power."

CHAPTER XXX.

LITTLE ROB IN CAPTIVITY.

Little Rob was a boy of delicate physique. He weighed but fifty six pounds, and was weaker than most boys of his age, but he had a courage which could hardly have been expected of his years. The discovery that he had been kidnaped startled him, but when he had time to reflect upon his situation he said to himself, "It's no use to cry. The men won't let me go any the sooner. I must see if I can't get away. If Frank only knew where I was, he would come and take me away."

Rob had great faith in Frank, ranking him next to his father.

"If I could only get a letter to Frank," he thought, "it would be all right."

Here, however, was a difficulty. He was locked in a small room in a part of the city which he had never before visited, and there seemed no chance to communicate with the outside world. Gerrish and Carter went out and left him alone. There were no books in the room, for the family were not literary, and Rob had no amusement except watching from the solitary window a goat disporting himself in the back yard.

At last the door opened, and the girl of sixteen whom Rob had seen when he entered the house came into the room with a small waiter, on which was a cup of tea and a plate of buttered bread. Her hair hung about her face in an unkempt mop, and there were spots of grease on her faded calico dress.

"I've brought you some vittles, Bob," she said.

"My name isn't Bob. It's Rob."

"The man said it was Bob, but it makes no odds. Do you feel hungry?"

"Yes, I do, thank you," answered little Rob politely.

"What do you thank me for?" asked the girl, staring.

"For your kindness in inquiring. I don't know when I've been so hungry."

"That's good. I'd have scared you up something better, only there wasn't no meat nor eggs in the house."

"I'm hungry enough to eat bread and butter," said Rob. "What is your name, if you don't mind telling me?"

"Why should I mind? My name's Stasia Jane."

"Stasia's a funny name. You don't mind my saying so, do you?"

"In course not. It is kind of queer. I disremember who I was named for. I was born and brung up in the country."

"Were you now? Wouldn't you rather be there than here?"

"I guess I would. Here I have to slave and slave, and all I get is my victuals and clo'es. Them's the clo'es," and she pointed scornfully at the greasy dress she had on.

"That is poor pay. Why do you stay?"

"Maybe I couldn't do no better."

"I think if I speak to Sarah—that's our cook—she might find you a better place."

"Why did you come here?" asked Stasia Jane abruptly. "You ain't come here to board, have you?"

"I've been stolen from home," said little Rob.

"Lawk a mercy! Did them men that brought you here steal you?"

"Yes, they did. Do you know them?"

"I've seen them before. They come here sometimes. What did they want to steal you for?"

"They think my papa will give a good deal of money to get me back."

"Has your papa, as you call him, got lots of money?"

"I think he has a good deal of money," said Rob, thoughtfully, "for we live in a big house in a nice street, but I don't know how much."

"Has he got as much as a thousand dollars, do you think?"

"I think he must have a good deal more than that."

"You don't say!" ejaculated Stasia Jane, regarding Rob with increased respect. "Do you think he'll pay these men to get you back?"

"I am sure he will, if he can't get me back any other way. I don't think it's right that they should get money for stealing me, do you?"

"I don't know. They was smart to do it."

"They are very wicked men. You know the oldest one—his name is Luke Gerrish. Well, he's been in prison for five years."

"Has he?" asked Stasia, not so much shocked as Rob expected, for she knew of others who had had a similar experience. "Has the young feller been there too?"

"I don't know. I think likely."

"Stasia Jane," said Rob, after a pause, "have you got any money?"

"Oh, law, no! I couldn't lend you a cent if 'twas to save your life."

"But I didn't want to borrow. I didn't suppose you would have any money to lend."

"Then what made you ask me?"

"Would you like to earn some money?"

"Well, I might."

"I want to write a letter to a friend, and I would like to have you send it for me."

"Would it make the men mad?"

"Yes; it would if they found out."

"How much would you give me?" asked Stasia Jane, becoming interested.

"A dollar."

"Certain true?" she asked eagerly.

"Yes."

"Have you got it?" she asked suspiciously.

In reply Rob drew out a silver dollar and showed it to her. She sounded it on the table, and the clear, ringing sound satisfied her that the coin was genuine.

"Well, where's the letter?" she asked.

"Is there any place near by where you can buy a sheet of note paper and an envelope?"

"Yes."

"Then please buy me one of each, and I'll write the letter. Here's five cents to pay for them. You can keep the change."

"All right!" said Stasia Jane with alacrity.

She took the money, and in five minutes brought back the required articles.

"I made three cents," she said complacently.

"I am glad you did. Now please tell me where I am."

"You're in this room," said Stasia Jane, staring at Rob as if his wits had gone astray.

"I mean the street and number."

"Oh, that's it. It won't get me into trouble with them men, will it?"

"They won't know you helped me. I won't tell them."

"They might step on my necktie if they found out."

"But you don't wear a necktie," said Rob, puzzled.

"Oh, well! you know what I mean."

"I don't see how they can find out. Just wait a minute and I'll have the letter ready."

Rob had a lead pencil in his pocket. He wrote this note rather slowly, and handed it to Stasia Jane:

DEAR FRANK: I have been stolen away by your stepfather and another man. They have locked me up in a back room at No. 179 Christopher Street. They want to make papa pay to get me back. I hope you will come and get me away. There is a girl here named Stasia Jane. She is a friend to me, and is a good girl, though she wears a dirty dress, and doesn't comb her hair. You can tell her you have come for me. Tell papa not to worry about me. I am sure the men won't hurt me. They only want money.

LITTLE ROB.

"Here is the letter," said Rob. "I wish you could take it to my house."

"I couldn't get away. If they found it out they'd kill me."

"Not really?" said Rob in alarm.

"No; but I'd get pounded, and perhaps I'd be sacked."

"What does that mean? They wouldn't put you in a sack, would they?"

"Lor, how precious green you are! I mean I'd be bounced."

"But you ain't a rubber ball. How could you be bounced?"

"What a little goose you are! I'd lose my job, and be turned out of the house."

"Oh, I see. What will you do, then?"

"I know a boy that lives next door—his name is Frank Sheehan. He'll go for a quarter."

"Here's the quarter," said little Rob, producing one from his pocket. "Tell him they'll give him more at the house."

Stasia Jane took the note and ran out without her bonnet. She espied Frank Sheehan playing marbles across the street, and beckoned him over.

"Here," she said, "you take this letter to where it is directed, and I'll give you a quarter."

"Where's the quarter?" asked Frank suspiciously.

"There it is!"

"It's a good way. I'll have to take the cars."

"Never you mind that! The folks will be glad to get it, and will pay you something extra."

Frank took the letter, and held it in his hand while walking up the street, studying the address. As Rob's ill luck would have it, he met Luke Gerrish, whose suspicions were aroused, though he did not know who wrote the letter.

"Give me that letter, Johnny," he said. "I think it's for me."

CHAPTER XXXI.

LITTLE ROB IS TRANSFORMED.

In his surprise Frank Sheehan handed Luke the letter.

"Aha, the little chap is foxy," he said, as he tore it open and took in the contents.

By this time the boy began to have misgivings.

"What made you open the letter?" asked Frank. "Give it back to me."

"Who gave you the letter?"

"I won't tell."

"Was it a boy?"

"Maybe it was."

Luke Gerrish became alarmed. Had Rob already escaped?

"What were you paid for carrying it?"

"A quarter."

"All right! You can keep the money. It's for me. So you won't have any trouble in carrying it."

Frank Sheehan was an average boy, and did not mind being saved a long walk.

"If they find out I didn't carry it they might want the money back," he said.

"They wouldn't know," said Luke, winking. "I won't tell, and I advise you not to. You can just go off the block for a couple of hours."

This struck Frank favorably, and he walked quickly on.

"The little rascal!" muttered Luke. "It's lucky I stopped his little game. I won't tell him, and he'll be watchin' and waitin' for my precious stepson to come and take him away. 'Tell papa not to worry,' he resumed, reading from the letter. 'I am sure the men won't hurt me. They only want money.' That's where the kid hit the nail on the head. They do want money, and they want it bad."

Luke went into the house, and, going up stairs, opened the door of the room in which little Rob was confined.

"Well, kid, are you glad to see me?" he asked, sitting down and crossing his legs.

"Yes, sir," answered little Rob, "if you've come to let me out."

"Sorry, my dear, but I couldn't part with you just yet. I dote on you, I do."

"I suppose that is a joke," said Rob, in a dignified tone. "Mr. Gerrish, won't you take me back to papa?"

"And what will papa pay me if I do?" asked Gerrish, with a cunning smile.

"I am sure that he will pay you something. I will ask him to give you ten dollars."

"Oho! it's you that are joking now, kid. I shall want ten thousand dollars at least."

"Ten thousand dollars!" repeated Rob in amazement. "I don't know as papa has so much money."

"Never you worry about that! He has that and a good deal more."

"You have no right to charge him money for getting me back."

"Look here, kid, you are too young to argue. Never mind whether it's right or not. The money must be paid."

"Frank will come and take me away," thought Rob, and this enabled him to keep up his courage. Luke Gerrish read this in his expressive countenance, and chuckled to himself as he thought of the way in which the little boy's letter had been intercepted. Still he felt that it was a narrow escape, and that some means must be taken to prevent communication between Rob and his home friends.

Carter arrived five minutes late, and Luke Gerrish, inviting him into the street for a short walk, asked his advice, first letting him know of the intercepted letter.

"There is another thing to consider," said Carter. "That boy of yours is no doubt on our track. "He is a smart boy, and foxy. He may already have got a clew."

"I'd like to mash him!" muttered Luke Gerrish.

"That's all very well, but if he finds the boy he'll be likely to get us into trouble."

"Well, if you've got through croaking," said Gerrish irritably, "tell me what you think we'd better do."

"We must leave this place," said Carter sententiously.

"Why?"

"It is too near to be safe. Besides, the boy has a friend here."

"How do you know that?"

"Some one provided him with the means of writing the note, and gave it to the messenger."

"Who do you think it is?"

"I don't know. Very likely it's the girl in the kitchen."

"I will question her."

"It will be of no use. She will of course deny it, and we can't prove it."

"Where shall we go?"

"We can think of that. There's one thing more. In his present dress the boy will be sure to excite suspicion in our company. You wouldn't dress your boy that way, nor I. He looks like the son of a rich man. We should be suspected of having stolen him."

"Perhaps you are right. What is your plan, if you have one?"

"We must tog him out as a poor boy or as a girl. A girl would be better, for he has long hair and looks delicate. We can call him Jane or Susan, and if he claims to be a boy say he is crazy."

"A good idea!" exclaimed Gerrish in a tone of satisfaction. "You're great at plotting, Carter. But where can we get girl's clothes? We haven't any money to spare."

"None is needed. Take off the boy's suit, and I will exchange it at some pawn shop for some girl's duds. When that's done I'll tell you what to do next."

Luke Gerrish assented readily. Though Carter was twenty years younger, he recognized him as his superior in brain capacity, and was willing to be led.

"But," he objected, "it will need money to go out of the city."

"Don't worry! On the strength of our prospects I have raised a small sum of money, enough to get through on."

Luke's face lighted up.

"You're a genius, Jack!" he said. "Give me half."

By way of answer, John Carter in a significant manner put his forefinger on one side of his nose.

"Couldn't think of it, Gerrish!" he said. "I prefer to be treasurer."

"Can't you trust me?" grumbled Gerrish in disappointment.

"Well, perhaps so," answered Carter dryly, "but I'd rather not try the experiment."

"The plan is mine, I ought to be leader."

"You may undertake the whole thing alone," said Carter, "if you prefer."

"No, no, I don't care to break away from you."

"Very well, then! Now we'll go up and get the boy's clothes."

As the two filed into the chamber Rob looked at them wistfully.

"Are you going to take me home?" he asked.

"Well, not just yet. You'll stay with us till your father comes down with ten thousand dollars."

"He won't pay so much money."

"Then he'll have to get along without you. Now take off your clothes, and get into bed."

"Why?" asked little Rob in surprise. "It isn't night."

"Never mind why. Do as I tell you."

"I would rather not, Mr. Gerrish."

"Then I will beat you so you can't stand," said Gerrish fiercely.

Looking in his face Rob felt afraid, and considering that after all it would not harm him, he obeyed orders.

"Now jump into bed."

The boy did so.

Carter gathered up the little boy's suit, made it into a parcel, and prepared to leave the room.

"Where are you going to carry my clothes?" asked little Rob in dismay.

"I'm going to have it cleaned and pressed," answered Carter jocosely.

Rob did not believe this, but he asked no further questions. He hoped that Frank would soon make his appearance, and then all his troubles would be over.

Two hours later Carter returned in company with Gerrish.

He had a small bundle in his hand, about the same size as the one he had taken away.

"You can dress yourself now, kid," said Gerrish with a grim smile.

Little Rob jumped out of bed with alacrity. If Frank came for him he wanted to be dressed, so that he could go away with him without delay.

Carter opened the bundle, and to the little boy's dismay drew out a small cheap dress, a petticoat, and a girl's hat.

"That's a girl's dress!" said little Rob, drawing back.

"Of course it is. You are going to be a little girl. Your name is Susie, can you remember that?"

Now no boy, however small, relishes the idea of masquerading as a girl. A look of real distress showed itself on Rob's face.

"No, no!" he said, "I don't want to wear girl's clothes."

"It won't make you a girl, you little fool!" said Gerrish harshly.

"But I don't want—"

"Jack, go down stairs and get a horsewhip!" said Gerrish frowning.

Little Rob made no further opposition, but allowed himself to be attired in girl's clothes. The dress altered him strangely. He still had a high bred expression, but so far as clothing went would readily have been taken for a poor girl like those who swarm in the crowded tenement house districts of New York.

CHAPTER XXXII.

LITTLE ROB LEAVES NEW YORK.

Early the next morning Stasia Jane was washing the front steps when the door was opened and Luke Gerrish, John Carter, and little Rob, the latter dressed as a girl, came out. Stasia Jane stared at Rob in amazement, not recognizing him, till the little boy said piteously, "Oh, Stasia Jane, they are taking me away."

"Shut up, kid!" said Luke Gerrish roughly. "Don't you dare to say a word, or I'll choke you!"

"Oh, my gracious goodness!" ejaculated Stasia Jane, dropping her scrubbing cloth in amazement. "You don't go for to say you're little Rob?"

"Yes, I am; they've dressed me up as a girl. If anybody comes for me tell them about it."

Luke Gerrish gave the little boy a savage shake.

"What did I tell you?" he exclaimed furiously. "I know all about your writing a letter yesterday. Here it is," and Gerrish grinning maliciously produced the note he had taken from Frank Sheehan. "You thought you'd played a trick upon me, did you? I wasn't born last week, as you'll find out. There won't be nobody calling for you, do you hear?"

Little Rob did hear, and the tears came to his eyes as he saw that his plan had failed.

"Where are you takin' him, mister?" asked Stasia Jane.

"Mind your own business, you ragbag," snarled Gerrish. "If anybody asks you, say you don't know."

"I never see such goin's on!" said Stasia Jane to herself. "Why have they dressed that poor little boy in gal's clothes? I'd like to know where they're goin'."

Then as she saw Frank Sheehan crossing the street, an inspiration came to her.

"Say, Frank, do you see them men with the little gal between them?"

"Well, what if I do?"

"It ain't a gal at all, it's a boy."

"You don't say?"

"Yes, I do—certain true."

"What did they do it for?"

"'Cause they've stolen him from his folks. His father's worth a hundred millions of dollars, and he'll pay an awful price to get him back. Don't you want some of it?"

"Yes, I do."

"Then go as fast as you can and find out where they're takin' him. I'll go and tell his folks, or you can, and they'll give us some money."

"You ain't foolin' me, be you?"

"No, I ain't. Don't stop to talk. Hurry along, and come back and tell me."

Frank Sheehan had nothing in particular to do, and he liked playing the detective. So he started on a run, but pulled up when he was about fifty feet distant from the party ahead. He took a knife from his pocket and began to whittle a stick. When Gerrish looked back to see if by chance he was followed, his glance rested on the boy, but Frank's face was so innocent of all expression that it never occurred to the kidnaper that the small boy was an amateur detective.

Presently the men boarded a horse car, and Frank was nonplused. He felt in his pocket, but could only find two pennies, and the car fare was five cents. But Frank had become interested in his detective work, and jumped on the car, resolved to take the chances of being put off.

It was five minutes before the conductor came round for his fare.

Frank plunged his hand into his pocket with a look of confidence, brought out the two pennies, shook his head, and began to explore his vest pockets. He put on an expression of solicitude and perplexity, and said in a tone of vexation, "Where did I put that nickel?"

"Hurry up, boy!" said the conductor impatiently. "I can't wait here all day."

"I don't see what can have become of it," murmured Frank.

"Either pay or get off!"

"Won't you let me ride and I'll pay you tomorrow?" pleaded the boy.

"No, I won't. We don't do business in that way. Come, hustle!"

Frank once more commenced exploring his pockets, but the conductor was by this time out of patience.

"Jump off!" he said, pulling the bell.

"Nay, friend," said a benevolent looking Quaker, "thee is too hasty! I will pay the boy's fare myself," and he handed the official a silver quarter.

"All right, sir, that settles it."

"Nay, give the boy the change," said the kindly Quaker.

"Young fellow, you're in luck!"

"I'm much obliged to you, sir," said Frank gratefully, as he pocketed the two dimes. "I'm in a great hurry, and didn't have time to walk."

"Thee is welcome. Don't spend the money foolishly."

"I won't, sir. I'll give it to my mother."

"That is right, my boy. Since thee is a good boy, here is fifty cents more for thee."

"I'm glad I came," thought Frank, after properly acknowledging the gift.

Presently Luke Gerrish signaled the conductor to stop.

When the car stopped he took little Rob by the hand, and got out, followed by Carter. Frank got out also but avoided looking at Rob and his abductors. He followed them across the street, and his eye lighted up with a look of intelligence.

"They're goin' to Albany," he decided as he saw the graceful outlines of the Albany day boat lying at the pier. But Frank was not satisfied with jumping at conclusions. He followed the party to the ticket office, and heard this conversation:

"I want to go to Albany," said Luke Gerrish. "You won't charge anything for the little gal, will you?"

"Half price," returned the official.

"You ought to let her go free," grumbled Gerrish.

"I must obey orders. How many tickets?"

"Two and a half."

The money was paid over, and the tickets shoved out. As Gerrish turned, Frank was looking in a different direction. Luke's suspicions were aroused.

"Look here, boy," he said roughly. "What do you want down here?"

"I want to go to Albany to see my sick aunt," said Frank boldly. "Won't you lend me a dollar?"

"Well, here's a cheek for you!" said Gerrish, turning to Carter. "Ain't you the boy that couldn't pay his fare on the horse cars?"

"Yes, sir."

"I suppose you've lost the dollar you were to buy the ticket to Albany with?" he continued in a sarcastic tone.

"I guess so, sir. There's a hole in my vest pocket."

"You're sly, but you ain't sly enough for me. I ain't no Broadbrim. You played it on the Quaker right smart, but Luke Gerrish is up to your tricks. Jack, that boy don't want to go to Albany. All he wants is the dollar."

"Looks like it," said Carter.

Frank Sheehan assumed an expression of chagrin.

"Then you won't give me the dollar?" he said.

"No, I won't, and I advise you to make yourself scarce, or I'll expose you as a humbug."

Frank had learned all he wanted, and was quite ready to go. He shrugged his shoulders, and going back to the street took a car up town.

"I guess I'll be a detective when I'm a little older," he said to himself complacently. "Now I'll go back and tell Stasia Jane what I've found out."

CHAPTER XXXIII.

FRANK MAKES PROGRESS.

Frank Manton spent the whole afternoon and part of the evening in a fruitless search for little Rob and his abductors. The more persons he interviewed the more bewildered he became. He had a talk with officer Grubb and officer Snow, who had been detailed to assist him. Officer Grubb snubbed him, and scouted all his suggestions as absurd.

"What does a boy like you know about detective business?" he said scornfully.

"Not much, perhaps," answered Frank. "Still I know something of the two men who carried little Rob away."

"You think you do!"

"I know more of Luke Gerrish than I wish I did, and something of John Carter."

"Your knowledge ought to be worth something," said officer Snow courteously.

"Nothing at all," said officer Grubb emphatically. "Now I have a theory."

"What is it?" asked his brother officer.

"I think the parties have gone to Boston."

"What reason have you for your belief?" asked officer Snow.

"I cannot tell you, but it is my conviction that we must seek for them in that direction."

"That is, you guess at it."

"Mr. Snow," said Grubb, "I trust you do not mean to insult me."

"By no means! Follow your clew if you have any, and I will seek elsewhere."

Officer Grubb went to the Grand Central Depot and kept vigilant watch of all who went in and out. Making inquiries of the gatemen he learned that two men and a small boy had bought tickets for Yonkers, and gone out by a train starting an hour earlier. He immediately took passage for the same place and spent the balance of the day in scouring Yonkers for the suspected parties, only to find about seven o'clock that they belonged to a well known family in the suburban city. In a disgusted frame of mind he returned to New York and reported "no discoveries."

Meanwhile Frank, by good luck, found the conductor of the Sixth Avenue car on which little Rob had taken passage. He traced them as far as Christopher Street—but there he lost the trail. The question arose, were they still in the city or had they crossed the ferry?

Frank was a young detective, and had no experience in past cases to assist him. It occurred to him, however, that some one in the neighborhood might have seen Rob and his abductors, and noticed where they went. He saw a group of boys playing, and without much hope of obtaining information, went up to them and inquired: "Did any of you see two men and a little boy coming down the street yesterday?"

One of the boys looked up quickly.

"Is your name Frank Manton?" he asked.

Of course the reader will understand that the speaker was Frank Sheehan.

"Yes," answered Frank astonished. "Do you know me?"

"I had a letter given me for you yesterday," answered the smaller boy.

"Why didn't you bring it to me?"

"Because a man took it away from me."

"But why did he take it away from you? What was the appearance of the man?"

Frank Sheehan gave a description which enabled Frank to identify the person referred to as Luke Gerrish.

He became excited, for he felt that he was getting on the track of Rob's abductor.

"I know the man," he said. "Did he have a little boy with him?"

"Is he your brother?" asked Frank Sheehan.

"No, but he was under my charge. Tell me all you know about him quick."

Frank Sheehan detached himself from the group of boys, and beckoned Frank aside.

"Stasia Jane told me you would pay us if we told you where to find the boy," he said.

"Who is Stasia Jane?"

"She lives at the house where the little boy was taken."

"Yes, you shall be well paid, both of you. Rob's father is rich, and he will pay you. Now where is he? Show me the house."

"I can show you the house, but the boy was took away this morning."

Frank was deeply disappointed. He thought he was on the point of finding Rob, and now he seemed farther off than ever.

"I'll take you round to see Stasia Jane," he said. "Maybe she can tell you more than I can."

Stasia Jane was in the kitchen, but quickly came out when Frank told her that a friend of the little boy was inquiring for him.

"Oh, why didn't you come yesterday?" she said. "Then you'd have got him before them wicked men took him away."

"When was he taken away?" asked Frank anxiously.

"Early this mornin'. When I saw them bring him down stairs dressed as a little gal, you might have knocked me down with a feather I was so s'prised."

"Did they dress him up as a girl?" asked Frank eagerly.

"Yes, they took off all his nice clo'es and made a gal out'n him. They are awful poor clo'es, not a bit better than these," and Stasia Jane glanced down at her own working dress, which had long since passed its best days.

Frank looked discouraged. He had found a clew only to lose it. He had discovered the house in which Rob was confined yesterday, but the bird was gone, and there was no evidence in what direction. So at least he thought.

"I'd give something to know where he was taken," he said soberly.

"Would you?" said Frank Sheehan eagerly. "Hand it over then."

"Can you tell me?"

"Yes; I follered 'em—Stasia Jane told me to. They've gone on board the Albany boat, and are goin' up the river as fast as they can."

"Is this true?" asked Frank, excited.

"Yes. I'll tell you all about it."

Frank Sheehan told his story, answering the questions that suggested themselves to the other Frank.

"This is very important," he said. "I must go to Albany at once."

"Don't forget to pay me!"

"And me," said Stasia Jane.

"I have only a little money with me, but I will give you a dollar each. You shall have a good deal more when Rob's father comes home from Chicago."

"Certain true?" asked Stasia Jane suspiciously.

"Yes. Let me take down your names, and I will come and pay you as soon as the boy is found."

The two saw their names put down with satisfaction. It seemed an assurance that Frank would act in good faith and his promise be kept.

Frank had now to consider what course to pursue. It would probably take nine hours for the boat to reach Albany. They were now at least two hours on the way. If Frank had been older he would have gone to police headquarters and got a telegram sent to the chief of police in Albany, requesting him to arrest the kidnapers on their arrival, but he was new to the detective business and this did not occur to him. He lost no time, however, in reaching the Grand Central Depot and taking passage on a train to Albany. He hoped to meet the boat on its arrival and snatch Rob from his abductors.

CHAPTER XXXIV.

ON THE HUDSON RIVER BOAT.

Under ordinary circumstances little Rob would have enjoyed a trip up the Hudson. It was a perfect day, and as the boat stopped at one landing after another the passengers had an opportunity of observing the charming scenery of this unsurpassed river.

Of course Luke Gerrish and Carter understood that there was danger of defeat to their plans in case Rob should communicate his situation to any of the passengers. They could not very well lock him up, unless they went to the expense of a stateroom, which in the present state of their finances they did not care to do. Luke thought best, however, to give Rob a warning.

"Look here, kid," he said, "I've got something to say to you."

"I wish you wouldn't call me 'kid,' Mr. Gerrish."

"Why not? Seems to me you're mighty particular."

"Because a kid is a young goat."

"So are you a young goat!" said Gerrish with an unpleasant smile. "Never mind about that! You're not to tell anybody who you are. Do you hear?"

"Yes, Mr. Gerrish, I hear, but I cannot promise that."

"What do you mean, hey?" demanded Luke, with an ugly frown.

"I mean that I want to get home to my papa, and perhaps some kind gentleman will help me if I tell them that you have stolen me from my home."

25. "I told you it was not a nice house."

26. "I've been stolen from home," said little Rob.

27. The dress altered Rob strangely.

28. "Look here, boy, what do you want down here?"

29. Stasia Jane and Frank Sheehan saw their names put down with satisfaction.

30. "Quite right, Gerrish. I see you are up to your old tricks."

31. "Can this be little Ro[...] asked Frank in amazeme[...]

32. Horatio Alger, Jr.

"Look here, kid! If you dare to tell anybody you've been stole I'll kill you."

"I don't think you will, Mr. Gerrish, for you would be hung."

"The little chap knows too much," muttered Gerrish. Then, as a new thought struck him, he said, "No, I won't kill you, but I'll take you to an insane asylum and shut you up among the crazy people."

"Oh don't do that, Mr. Gerrish!" pleaded little Rob, horror struck.

Luke smiled grimly. He congratulated himself on having struck the right key note at last.

"You'll be all right if you keep your tongue still," he said. "If you don't——" and he made a significant pause.

Little Rob had always had a horror of insanity. Once when walking in Central Park with his nurse at the age of six a crazy man had sprung at him and seized him by the throat, glaring murderously at the timid child. He had never forgotten the horror of this attack, and it was vivid in his mind today when Luke Gerrish made his threat.

"I should die if you shut me up among crazy people!" he faltered.

"It'll be your own fault if I do," said Gerrish.

Both Luke and Carter found it wearisome to look constantly after their young charge. After seeing the effect of his threat Luke concluded that it would be unnecessary to do so.

"The boy won't dare to peach," he said to Carter, and he laughed as he spoke of Rob's horror at the prospect of being consigned to an asylum.

"Stay where you are, kid!" he said, as he and Carter started to go down on the lower deck. "Mind what I told you, and don't say a word to anybody."

Poor Rob stood by the railing and looked sadly at the shore. Every moment was taking him farther and farther away from his father and Frank. When would he ever see them again?

Where would these wicked men take him? As these sad thoughts passed through his mind, the tears unbidden rose to his eyes.

A tall young man was pacing the deck with a young lady, evidently his sister from the resemblance. They were fond of children, and the sight of the forlorn little girl shedding tears roused their compassion.

"Walter," said Marcia Perkins, "how miserable that poor little girl looks! I am going to speak to her."

CHAPTER XXXV.

ROB FINDS FRIENDS.

Walter Perkins was a young actor who was on his way to Albany
to fill an engagement at one of the theaters there. His sister
accompanied him, having a school friend whom she proposed
to visit. Both were fond of children, and little Rob's forlorn
attitude and evident sorrow impressed them with compassion.
They had noticed also Luke Gerrish, and were surprised that
a person like him should have a child in his charge of so refined
a type as little Rob, whom they supposed from his appearance
to be a girl.

"Are you not feeling well, little girl?" asked Marcia Perkins
kindly.

"I am not a little girl," answered Rob, looking up gratefully
to the kind face bent over him.

The young lady looked puzzled.

"You are not a little girl?" she repeated.

"No."

"What are you, then?" asked Walter.

"I am a little boy."

"Then why are you dressed in girls' clothes?"

"Because the man that took me away from home does not
want it known that I am a boy."

"The man that took you from home? Is it the man we saw
speaking to you a little while ago?"

"Yes; his name is Luke Gerrish, and he is a bad man."

"Do you mean that he has stolen you from home?"

"Yes."

"Walter," said his sister, "this is an incident in real life quite equal to any in your plays."

"True."

"Can't we do anything for the little—boy? This man must be very bold."

"What is your name?" asked the young actor.

"Robert Palmer—they call me little Rob—that is, papa does, and Frank."

"Do you live in New York city?"

"Yes; in West 48th Street."

"Are you related to Mr. Allen Palmer, the banker?"

"I am his son."

"Well, this is indeed an adventure!" said Walter Perkins. "Do you know where this man is taking you?"

"There are two men—Luke Gerrish and John Carter. They are down stairs. I am afraid they will come up and see me talking to you."

"Would they treat you roughly?"

"He—Luke Gerrish—says if I tell any one who I am he will have me put in an asylum with crazy people;" and Rob's face showed the terror with which the threat had inspired him.

"Don't be alarmed! I will see that he doesn't do it. He only said so to frighten you. Have you any idea why he has stolen you?"

"Yes; he says he won't give me back unless papa gives him ten thousand dollars."

"Why, it is another Charlie Ross case!" said Marcia Perkins. "Can't we do anything to stop this man?"

"I have made up my mind to stop him. If the little boy will tell me his story, and all the particulars of his abduction, I can tell better how to act."

"He's coming on deck!" interrupted little Rob nervously, as he glanced toward the staircase leading up from below.

Walter Perkins and his sister took the hint, and resumed their walk, carefully refraining from looking at Rob.

"Well, kid, how goes it?" demanded Gerrish. "How do you like the trip?"

"It's very pleasant," said Rob, looking more cheerful, his hopes being excited by the new friends he had made. "Will you send me home when we get to Albany?"

"If you are a good—girl, and your father comes to time. Don't look so stupid, or people will suspect something. Go round, and look lively."

"All right, Mr. Gerrish!"

Luke Gerrish went down stairs and rejoined Carter.

"The kid's all right. He's looking more chipper than he did," said he. "We don't need to bother about him."

"I'm glad of that. It's a nuisance having charge of a child."

"But it's going to pay, eh, Carter?" said Gerrish significantly.

"I hope so. I haven't got much more money left, Gerrish."

"I suppose Frank is hunting all over New York for the kid. His stepfather's a little too smart for him this time," chuckled Luke Gerrish.

Again the young actor and his sister joined Rob.

"Walter," said the young lady, "we must hide our little friend in some way, so that these men cannot find him. Suppose you hire a stateroom and I will go in there with him till the boat reaches Albany."

"A good suggestion. I will go and secure one at once."

On the day boats there is no difficulty in obtaining a stateroom. Most passengers do not care for one, but occasionally some one has a headache, or wishes to lie down, and finds it convenient to have the exclusive use of a room.

The young actor returned to his sister.

"This is the key to No. 19," he said. "You and the boy can go in there now, if you like."

"I think we had better do so," said Marcia. "I have some books with me which will help entertain him. Perhaps I had better not remain too long, or I may be missed from the deck, and his companions may suspect that we have had something to do with his disappearance."

"Well thought of! I will go to the head of the staircase and see that neither of his captors is near, while you lead him to the stateroom."

"Come with me, or rather follow close behind me," said Marcia in a low tone. "Between us I think we can get you away from these wicked men."

Rob followed a few steps behind, and in less than ten minutes was ensconced in stateroom No. 19.

"You can lie down if you like," said Marcia.

"I think I will, for I am tired," said little Rob. "I did not sleep very well last night."

"Do you think you could fall asleep? It might do you good."

"I think I might. You are sure Luke Gerrish won't find me?"

"I don't see how he can."

Satisfied with her assurance Rob lay down in the comfortable berth, and was soon fast asleep. His delicate face looked thinner and more careworn as the result of the trying ordeal through which he had passed. Marcia Perkins remained with him till she judged by his deep regular breathing that he was asleep, and then softly retiring locked the door on the outside. She had warned Rob that she would do this in the interest of his safety, so that if he waked up he might not be frightened at finding he was locked in.

Luke Gerrish and John Carter remained below, quite easy in mind as to the safety of their charge. At length Carter went up stairs and looked carefully round, but did not see Rob. A little startled, he walked hurriedly from one end of the deck to the other, but nothing could be seen of the stolen child.

He went down stairs hurriedly.

"Luke," said he, "I can't see anything of the kid."

"Oh, he's somewhere on deck. I told him to walk round."

"I have looked everywhere, and cannot find him."

Luke Gerrish did not reply, but went up stairs in haste.

"If he's hidin' away I'll give him a touch of the stick," he said. But he looked in vain for the boy. His anxiety increased.

"You don't think he'd jump overboard, do you, Carter?" he asked hoarsely.

"No; if he had, some one would have seen him, and there would have been a fuss made."

"He couldn't have got off at one of the stopping places?"

"If he had I should have seen him. I thought of that, and kept on the watch."

The two men searched through the large boat, but, as they could not see into the staterooms, of course they did not discover the lost boy.

"You ought to have kept him with you all the time, Gerrish," said Carter, reproachfully. "If you had, this wouldn't have happened."

"I ought, ought I?" snarled Gerrish, who always resented fault finding. "Why not you as well as I?"

"Well, perhaps I had. But I guess it'll all turn out right. The boy must be on board somewhere. He'll turn up before we get to Albany."

"I hope so, or we'll both be in the soup. It puzzles me where he can have sneaked to."

A young man with light side whiskers came up to Luke Gerrish.

"Are you looking for the little girl I saw you speaking with an hour or two since?" he asked.

"Yes; do you know where she is?" returned Luke eagerly.

"I saw that young man and his sister talking with her for quite a good while. Then the young lady took her away."

"Ha! it's a case of abduction, is it?" said Luke indignantly. "I'll have them both arrested for stealin' away my little gal!" and he strode up to the young actor wrathfully.

CHAPTER XXXVI.

LITTLE ROB'S ESCAPE.

"What have you done with my little gal?" demanded Luke Gerrish gruffly, as he paused in front of the young actor.

Young Perkins returned the gaze of the bully, who towered above him, without betraying any evidence of alarm.

"I haven't the pleasure of knowing you, sir," he answered.

"You ain't, hey? Well, you'll be likely to know more of me than you want to."

"I already know more of you than I care to. Please stand out of the way."

"That won't do! I want to know what you have done with my little gal."

"Have you a little girl?" asked the young man pointedly.

"Why of course I have. You saw me up here talkin' to her."

"Yes, I saw the one you mention. You are willing to swear that it is a little girl?"

"Look here!" said Gerrish suspiciously, "what has she been telling you?"

"That she isn't a girl at all, but a boy."

"Oh, that's it, is it?" said Gerrish, laughing uneasily. "The poor thing is crazy, and doesn't know what she says."

"She's your child?"

"Why, of course she is! Now tell me where she is."

"I would rather not."

By this time several passengers had gathered about the two speakers.

"You know where she is?" said Luke aggressively.

"Yes, I know."

"And you won't tell me?"

"It's a shame!" said an elderly woman with more sentiment than sense. "What right have you to take away the child from her poor father?"

"That's what I say!" chimed in a red faced man, pounding the deck with his heavy cane. "It's a clear case of abduction. My friend," this was addressed to Gerrish, "I advise you to have this young man arrested."

"I thought you'd sympathize with me, sir," said Luke, taking a dirty handkerchief from his pocket and drying on it some imaginary tears. "It's hard on a poor father—an honest, hard working man—to have a city dude steal his little child."

"So it is, it is!" observed the elderly female, appearing much affected.

Walter Perkins felt that he was being unfavorably regarded by the majority of the passengers, and he flushed a little, although he felt that he was in the right.

"Is there any person on board who will confirm your statement that the child belongs to you?" he asked.

"Why yes, of course."

"Call him, then."

Luke Gerrish went down stairs to the lower deck, and quickly reappeared with John Carter.

"Jack," he said, "this chap here wants to know if the little gal belongs to me."

"Of course she does," said Carter, a trifle uneasily.

"There!" said Gerrish triumphantly. "You hear that, ladies and gentlemen. Now, I ask you, am I to have my rights or not?"

"Give up the child!" said half a dozen voices.

There was a shade of menace in the words. It is the custom with Americans to take sides promptly, often on insufficient evidence.

"Walter," said his sister Marcia rather alarmed, "perhaps you had better do so, and take other steps afterwards."

"What!" exclaimed the young actor, "give up the poor child into the hands of that ruffian? I will go and speak with the captain, and if he advises me to do it I will be guided by him."

The captain was on the lower deck. Young Perkins sought him out, and said, "Captain, are you aware that among your passengers are a couple of kidnapers, having in charge the only son of a wealthy New York banker?"

The captain was instantly interested.

"Give me the particulars," he said briefly.

The young actor did so.

"What does the man say?"

"That the child is crazy."

"Do you believe it?"

"No; I would like to bring you face to face with the child, and let you judge for yourself."

"Where is the child?"

"In my stateroom—No. 19."

The captain at once proceeded to the stateroom, and asked several questions which little Rob answered intelligently.

"Do you know who this man is that has abducted you?" asked the captain.

"Yes, it is Luke Gerrish."

"What do you know of him?"

"That he lately came from Sing Sing prison, where he was confined for five years."

"Ah!" said the captain thoughtfully. "That is important, if true. Fortunately I have on board an ex-official of the prison, who is confined to his stateroom with a headache. Probably he will be able to identify this Gerrish."

"Mr. Maitland," said the captain, entering the stateroom of the official referred to, "do you remember any convict at Sing Sing during your stay there named Luke Gerrish?"

"Very well. He is a hard case. Why?"

"He is on board this boat. He has a young child in charge who claims to be the son of Allen Palmer, the rich banker."

"Case of kidnaping!" said Mr. Maitland curtly.

"Yes; he claims the child is his. Now if you can identify him——"

"Of course I can. Shall I go with you now?"

"Yes, if you please."

Luke Gerrish was on the deck, posing for sympathy. It occurred to him that as an honest, hard working man, with a crazy child to support, he might draw a few dollars from the sympathetic, but indiscriminating crowd of passengers whom he had imposed upon by his sham tears.

"I have spent a great deal of money on the little gal!" he said, whining. "I don't care for myself, as long as she lives comfortable."

"Poor man!" said the elderly lady, wiping away a tear. "I am not rich, but here is a dollar if it will do you any good."

"May God bless you, ma'am, for a charitable lady!" said Luke fervently.

"And here's another dollar!" added the red faced man. "My good man, I feel that you have been basely used by this young man," and he glared vindictively at Walter Perkins. "There are some here who can sympathize with you."

"Oh, if all the rich were like you two," said the delighted Luke, "the lot of the poor laboring man would be less bitter. Would it not, Jack?"

"It would indeed," said Carter, privately deciding that one of the dollar bills belonged by right to him.

All things seemed to go swimmingly with the two kidnapers when the captain came up, followed at a little distance by Mr. Maitland.

"Oh, captain!" said the elderly lady, gushingly, "please make that bad young man give up the child to its poor father. It is a wicked shame to have a child stolen, and right on board your boat too."

The captain smiled slightly, and addressed himself to Luke Gerrish.

"You claim the child as yours, do you?" he asked.

"Yes, sir."

"Where do you live?"

"In—in Trenton, when I am at home. But I go out to work lately, and am on my way to Albany to see if I can find something to do there."

"How long were you employed at your last place?"

"F—five years!" answered Gerrish hesitatingly.

"Quite right, Gerrish!" said an unexpected voice, which made Luke turn swiftly. "Only it wasn't at Trenton, it was at Sing Sing you were employed. I see you are up to your old tricks. If you are on this boat when we reach Albany, I can secure you return tickets to your old home."

Luke Gerrish turned pale. He had no difficulty in recognizing Maitland, and he felt the game was up. He slunk down stairs, followed by Carter.

"Oh, what is this terrible thing?" asked the elderly lady, clasping her black mitted hands.

"Nothing, madam, except that you have been wasting your sympathy and money on a State's prison convict, and done all you could to assist him in carrying out his plan of kidnaping the son of a wealthy banker."

The old lady looked very much confused and ashamed, but forgot to apologize to the young actor for the hard things she had said of him.

"Now that it is safe," said Walter Perkins, "I will produce the child."

He went to the stateroom, and soon reappeared, holding little Rob by the hand.

At the next landing two passengers—Luke Gerrish and John Carter—hastily disembarked. Little Rob, standing by the railing, saw them leave and vanish up the pier with a sense of relief. He felt that his troubles were nearly over.

CHAPTER XXXVII

HOW ROB WAS FOUND.

When Frank took his seat on a train bound for Albany, his heart was filled with anxiety, and he did not for some time examine his fellow passengers. When he did so, he was destined to a surprise. Two seats ahead of him, and sitting alone, was his old employer, Silas Snobden.

Frank was pleased to meet an old acquaintance. He went forward at once, and, holding out his hand, said, "Good morning, Mr. Snobden."

The old gentleman looked up, and recognized Frank in some surprise.

"Why, it is Frank!" he said. Then, noticing critically his old office boy's improved appearance, he said, "Have you a new place?"

"Yes, sir; two."

"How can that be?" asked the merchant, puzzled.

"I work in the daytime for one party, and in the evening for another."

"You are lucky. Do you know, I am sorry you left me. I haven't been as well suited since."

"I am glad to hear you say that, Mr. Snobden, but," Frank added with a smile, "if you remember, I only left you because I was discharged."

"I was hasty in discharging you," admitted Mr. Snobden.

"How were you pleased with Benson Tyler?" asked Frank.

"He was caught stealing stamps," answered Silas Snobden curtly. "I did not have him arrested out of respect for his uncle, who is one of my oldest clerks."

"I know, sir—Mr. Chapin."

"His uncle has been trying to get me to take him back, but it is quite out of the question. If you wish to come back you can begin next Monday."

"Thank you, sir, but it would not do to leave my present employers."

Mr. Snobden's respect for Frank seemed to increase when he found that he no longer cared to return to his office.

"But," he said, "how do you happen to be traveling today? That isn't in the line of your duties, is it?"

"No, sir, not commonly, but I am in trouble. I was left in charge of the son of Mr. Allen Palmer, the banker, during his father's visit to Chicago. During my absence the boy was kidnaped, and I am in search of him."

"Mr. Palmer intrusted you with the charge of his son!" exclaimed Mr. Snobden in amazement.

"Yes, sir; the boy took a fancy to me, and I have been his evening companion for weeks."

"Yet you allowed him to be kidnaped?" said Snobden sharply.

"It was not my fault. It happened while I was not at the house."

"Have you any clew to the party who kidnaped him?"

"There were two parties implicated. I know them both."

"It is hardly to your credit to be acquainted with gentlemen in that line of business."

"One is a connection of mine, the other is a relation of yours."

"John Carter?" inquired Mr. Snobden quickly.

"Yes; I learn that it was he who lured little Rob away from home. My stepfather was waiting at the corner of the street, and the two carried off the poor little fellow."

"But you have some information as to where they took him?"

"Yes, sir; they are at this moment on the day line boat for Albany. I shall arrive there before the boat, and will wait for them at the pier with a policeman."

"And you took this step without advising with any one?"

"Yes, sir."

"Frank, you are a smart boy!" said the merchant admiringly. "I see now what a fool I was to part with you on account of a silly charge."

"I hope you don't still think that I play poker?" said Frank with a smile.

"No, I don't."

"Thank you, sir. I am glad to be vindicated at last. Are you going all the way to Albany?"

"Yes; and as my business is not pressing I will go with you to the pier to see my graceless nephew in his new role of rascality."

"I shall be very glad of your company, sir."

As we know, Mr. Snobden and Frank were both doomed to disappointment. Luke Gerrish and John Carter, for reasons already referred to, left the boat forty miles south of Albany, and were not on board when it reached the pier.

Frank and Mr. Snobden waited impatiently while the boat was being made fast, and both watched scrutinizingly the passengers as they disembarked. But there was no sign of the kidnapers, and, a still more bitter disappointment, there was no one that looked like little Rob. Frank's glance fell casually on a young man and woman who led between them a shabbily dressed little girl, and it occurred to him as rather strange that so well dressed a pair should allow their child to be so poorly clothed.

"I don't see anything of the boy," said Frank regretfully. "I am afraid he must have been taken off the boat at some landing below."

"It is Frank!" exclaimed a childish voice that thrilled our hero. Little Rob had just discovered him.

Frank looked about him in bewilderment. It was certainly Rob's voice, but where was he?

Turning he saw the shabby little girl, with her eyes fixed earnestly, longingly, upon him.

"Can this be little Rob?" asked Frank in amazement.

"Yes, Frank. They dressed me up as a little girl, and they would have carried me off, if it hadn't been for Mr. Perkins."

The young actor drew a card from his pocket, and presented it with a bow.

"I am Walter Perkins, an actor by profession," he said. "I am glad to have been of service to your young charge, and am pleased to surrender him to his friends."

"Thank you," said Frank gratefully. "Your service will not be forgotten. Are Rob's kidnapers among the passengers?"

"No; they found it convenient to leave the boat, some forty miles back."

"I am sorry," said Mr. Snobden. "I wanted to meet my graceless nephew. I have a debt to pay him. The blow he dealt me in my office I mean he shall suffer for some time. One thing is sure: the worthless vagabond shall not inherit one cent of my estate. I would rather leave my money to my office boy."

"Meaning me, sir?" asked Frank with a smile.

"Yes," was the unexpected reply. "I wish you were my nephew instead of John Carter. He is a disgrace to any family."

"Gentlemen," said Walter Perkins, "I shall be obliged to leave you, as I must report at the theater. If you remain in Albany long enough, I shall be glad to see you there."

"Thank you, Mr. Perkins, but I shall spend the night quietly with Rob at a hotel. When you return to New York his father will be glad to have you call that he may thank you in person for your kindness to his son."

"Frank," said little Rob, "I am ashamed of this dirty girl's dress. Won't you buy me some boy's clothes?"

"What did Luke Gerrish do with your suit?"

"He sold it, I expect."

Frank looked rather embarrassed. "I am afraid Rob," he said, "that I shall have to wait till we get back to New York. I didn't have a chance to go to your father's banking house to draw any money, and I have only about enough to pay our hotel bill and get us home."

"No matter," said little Rob, stifling a sigh as he looked with aversion at the shabby and dirty dress, "I can wait."

"You need not wait," said Silas Snobden. "As my graceless nephew is partly responsible for your troubles, the least I can do is to lend you money enough to replace the suit. Here is twenty five dollars, Frank. Use it judiciously, and Mr. Palmer can repay it when he returns to the city."

"I shall be glad to accept the loan, Mr. Snobden," said Frank. "I will myself call and repay you within a week. Can you recommend me a good hotel?"

"I generally go to the Delavan House."

The party took a carriage to the Delavan, and after taking rooms Frank procured the address of a dealer in boy's clothing, and little Rob, much to his relief, soon found himself arrayed in a velvet suit quite as good as the one he had lost.

"I don't want to be a girl again," he said. "It is much better fun to be a boy."

Frank remembered the anxious household in Forty Eighth Street, and sent the following telegram.

LITTLE ROB IS SAFE WITH ME. I SHALL BRING HIM HOME TOMORROW.

FRANK.

CHAPTER XXXVIII.

CONCLUSION.

Mr. Allen Palmer drove up to his own door in a hack fifteen minutes before the arrival of Frank's telegram, having been able to leave Chicago earlier than he anticipated. His face was beaming, for he was enjoying the prospect of meeting little Rob after what had seemed to him a very long absence from home.

He rang the bell, which was answered by Katy.

The poor girl looked sad, for nothing had been heard of the lost boy, and she and the cook were very anxious.

"Oh, goodness gracious!" she exclaimed, when she saw Mr. Palmer.

"You are surprised to see me, Katy!" said the banker, smiling. "I got away sooner than anticipated."

"Yes, sir," answered Katy mechanically. "Oh! how shall I tell him?" she said to herself.

"How is little Rob? Is he well?"

"I hope so, sir," faltered Katy.

"You hope so? Surely you know. Send him to me."

"I would, sir, but——"

"But what?"

"He isn't in the house."

"Oh, he is out with Frank, I suppose. Have they gone to Central Park?"

"No, sir."

"Really, Katy, you are very mysterious. Rob is not sick, is he?"

"I don't think so, sir. I—I don't know."

Mr. Palmer set down his valise and eyed Katy sharply.

"If there is anything to tell," he said, "tell it to me, and tell me quickly."

"Then I will, sir, though it breaks my heart! Little Rob's been stole away!"

"WHAT!" exclaimed Mr. Palmer, staggering as if he had received a blow. "Who has done this? When did it happen? Why did Frank allow it?" and his face became stern, as he thought it might have happened through Frank's negligence.

"It happened yesterday morning, sir, before Master Frank arrived."

Mr. Palmer managed with some difficulty to obtain from Katy the particulars as they are already known to the reader.

"And where is Frank?" asked the father.

"He's gone after little Rob."

"Has he any clew? Did he find out who took the poor little fellow?"

"Yes, sir; he says there were two men. He knows them both."

"Did he mention their names?"

"Luke Gerrish and John Carter. He says they took him to get money out of you."

"Has he given notice to the police?"

"Yes, sir; there are two men put on the case, but he has found out something they don't know, and he started for Albany this morning."

"Good! I would have staked my life on the fidelity of that boy. Oh, Rob! Rob! I never expected such a home coming as this!" and the stricken father dropped into a chair in utter prostration.

There was a sharp ring at the door bell.

Katy left the room to answer it, and quickly returned with an air of excitement.

"It's a telegram, sir!" she said.

"Give it to me!"

Mr. Palmer tore open Frank's dispatch, and his face was radiant.

"Listen to this, Katy!" he said. "Little Rob has been found, and Frank will bring him home tomorrow."

"Oh, glory, glory!" exclaimed Katy, throwing up her hands in ecstasy. "May I go and tell cook, sir?"

"Yes, go and tell her at once. After all, this is a happy day. Frank has indeed proved a treasure. His service in recovering little Rob shall not be forgotten!"

Mr. Palmer did not go to his banking house the next day. He waited impatiently, till about noon Frank arrived, leading little Rob by the hand. It was a wonder the boy was not suffocated as one after another embraced him.

"Frank," said Mr. Palmer, clasping the hand of our hero in a firm pressure, "you have proved a true friend to me and mine. You shall not lose by it. You shall tell me everything that happened later on. Now we must see that you and Rob are made comfortable."

"Rob has been complaining of feeling tired," said Frank. "I think it will do him good to go to bed and rest quietly."

The little boy did indeed look fatigued. His eyes were heavy, and he was paler than usual. His strength had been overtaxed, and the result was an attack of sickness, which grew more and more serious, till the banker became alarmed lest his son had only been restored to be taken from him by a foe more dangerous even than kidnapers. There were two weeks of anxious watching, in which Frank bore his part.

One night, when his father was at his bedside, little Rob fixed his eyes gravely on his face.

"Papa!" he said.

"Well, Rob?"

"I want to ask a favor of you."

"Surely, Rob!"

"If I shouldn't get well——"

"But, Rob," said his father in alarm, "you don't feel any worse, do you?"

"No, papa; I hope I shall get well, but if I don't I want you to promise to give Frank some of the money you meant for me."

"There is no need of promising. I made up my mind when Frank brought you back that I would provide for him. He shall never want a friend as long as you and I live, Rob."

"Thank you, papa!" and Rob put out his little hand and clasped his father's with a grateful pressure. "I think I will try to live, for I want to see Frank happy and prosperous."

Frank knew nothing of this conversation, but when Rob was out of danger, and was able to sit up once more, Mr. Palmer called him into the library.

"Well, Frank," he said, "the doctor says Rob will soon be up again."

"I am very much relieved to hear it," said Frank earnestly.

"I am sure of that. You are very much attached to little Rob," and the banker's face grew soft and his tone gentle.

"Yes; I love him like a brother."

"And he loves you. In his name, and at his request, I give you this," and Mr. Palmer drew from his pocket an unsealed envelope.

Opening it mechanically Frank looked bewildered when he saw that it contained a certified check for

TEN THOUSAND DOLLARS.

"Is this for me?" he asked in amazement.

"Yes, for I know you will make good use of it."

"How can I thank you, sir?" exclaimed Frank, in a burst of gratitude. "There will be no more poverty, no more hard work for my mother."

"Yes, Frank, it is your duty to make things easy for her. She has been your best friend. But keep the money in your own hands. Remember that you have a stepfather who has no claim upon you, but who might give your mother trouble."

"Thank you, sir. May I go home and tell mother of my good fortune?"

"Certainly."

"And would you keep and invest this money for me?"

"I will do so, and allow you six per cent interest, payable monthly. I will also take you into my banking house at a salary, to begin on, of ten dollars a week. But it will be necessary for you to give up your place with the historian."

"He can easily get some one to fill it. I think I would rather become a banker than a historian."

"There is probably more money in it," said Mr. Palmer with a smile.

When Frank reached home he could hardly make his mother believe in his good fortune. There was great joy in the humble household, but it was then and there decided that what had been a suitable home for Silas Snobden's office boy would never do for a banker's clerk, worth ten thousand dollars. A neat flat was taken up town and partially newly furnished. They had scarcely occupied it a week when one evening the door opened and Luke Gerrish staggered in.

"Upon my word, Mrs. G.!" he ejaculated, "you have become a fine lady. I think I'll come and live here."

"Mr. Gerrish," said Frank resolutely, "you must leave this place at once."

"Must I, indeed? And who's got a better right here than I? Ain't I your mother's husband?"

"Yes, I am sorry to say. But the flat is mine, and I pay for it. My mother is my guest; you are not."

"I mean to stay all the same," said Gerrish in a tantalizing way.

"Excuse me a minute, mother."

Frank left the room and found a policeman.

"Please come up stairs with me," he said. "Here is a warrant for the arrest of Luke Gerrish, lately released from Sing Sing, on a charge of kidnaping."

"All right," said the policeman.

Gerrish was sitting back in an easy chair eying his wife with a smile of lazy self complacence.

"On my word," he said, "we'll live here mighty snug, Mrs. G. As for that kid of yours, I'll have to take him in hand."

"This is his flat," said Mrs. Manton. "You cannot stay here."

"We'll see!" returned Gerrish, nodding his head. "Who's a goin' to put me out, that's what I'd like to know?"

He was soon answered.

Frank entered with an officer.

"That's the man," he said, pointing out Luke Gerrish.

"You must come with me," said the officer, laying his hand on Luke's shoulder.

"What for? This is my home and my wife."

"Can't help it! I have a warrant for your arrest on the charge of kidnaping the son of Allen Palmer, the banker."

Luke's face fell.

"I don't know anything about the boy," he said. "This is a conspiracy."

"All right! You can show it in court."

Luke Gerrish had to go *nolens volens*, and in due time he was tried and sentenced to several years' imprisonment on the charge preferred. John Carter, who was captured the next day, shared his captivity. When Luke is released he will be tried on another charge, that of robbing a countryman in Albany, and it is safe to say it will be many years before he can again trouble Frank or his mother.

I understand that "The History of the Saracens" will be published the present year, and that Frank's name will appear in the preface as a collaborator. Silas Snobden has become quite attached to his former office boy, and it is thought that Frank will come in for a good legacy when he dies. Gideon Chapin has lost his position, and has been obliged to accept one at a smaller salary in Brooklyn. Benson Tyler at nineteen is earning only five dollars a week, and making his mother's life uncomfortable by his fretfulness. He is very respectful to Frank now, and has several times borrowed five dollars of him, which it is needless to say is likely to prove a permanent investment.

As for Frank, all goes smoothly with him. He is diligent in business, and is likely to become a rich man.